"Hello, you've reached the voice mail of Lila Maxwell at Collette, Inc. I'm not available right now, so please leave a message and I'll get back to you soon. Thanks—and have a great day! [Beep]"

[You have one message from Jayne Randolph, extension 555, left today at 9:05 a.m.]

"Hi, Lila, it's me—Jayne. Just wanted to get your thoughts on last night's bachelorette auction. Did Meredith look incredible up there or what? Not to mention the way that supersexy bachelor Adam Richards was looking at her. The chemistry between them was so obvious, I thought Adam was going to hop onto the stage and make her a bid she couldn't refuse. I think this guy is perfect for Meredith, and she does deserve the best. Anyway, thought I'd give you a ring and we could discuss Meredith's extraordinary transformation. Call me later, or stop by—I'll be home. Bye!"

Dear Reader,

Welcome to Silhouette Desire, where every month you can count on finding six passionate, powerful and provocative romances.

The fabulous Dixie Browning brings us November's MAN OF THE MONTH, *Rocky and the Senator's Daughter,* in which a heroine on the verge of scandal arouses the protective *and* sensual instincts of a man who knew her as a teenager. Then Leanne Banks launches her exciting Desire miniseries, THE ROYAL DUMONTS, with *Royal Dad*, the timeless story of a prince who falls in love with his son's American tutor.

The Bachelorette, Kate Little's lively contribution to our 20 AMBER COURT miniseries, features a wealthy businessman who buys a date with a "plain Jane" at a charity auction. The intriguing miniseries SECRETS! continues with *Sinclair's Surprise Baby*, Barbara McCauley's tale of a rugged bachelor with amnesia who's stunned to learn he's the father of a love child.

In *Luke's Promise* by Eileen Wilks, we meet the second TALL, DARK & ELIGIBLE brother, a gorgeous rancher who tries to respect his wife-of-convenience's virtue, while *she* looks to *him* for lessons in lovemaking! And, finally, in Gail Dayton's delightful *Hide-and-Sheikh*, a lovely security specialist and a sexy sheikh play a game in which both lose their hearts…and win a future together.

So treat yourself to all six of these not-to-be-missed stories. You deserve the pleasure!

Enjoy,

Joan Marlow Golan

Joan Marlow Golan
Senior Editor, Silhouette Desire

THE BACHELORETTE

KATE LITTLE

Published by Silhouette Books
America's Publisher of Contemporary Romance

Special thanks and acknowledgment are given to Kate Little for her contribution to the 20 AMBER COURT series.

ISBN 0-373-76401-4

THE BACHELORETTE

This edition published by arrangement with Harlequin Books S.A.

Visit Silhouette at www.eHarlequin.com

Printed in U.S.A.

Books by Kate Little

Silhouette Desire

Jingle Bell Baby #1043
Husband for Keeps #1276
The Determined Groom #1302
The Millionaire Takes a Bride #1349
The Bachelorette #1401

KATE LITTLE

claims to have lots of experience with romance—"the *fictional* kind, that is," she is quick to clarify. She has been both an author and an editor of romance fiction for over fifteen years. She believes that a good romance will make the reader experience all the tension, thrills and agony of falling madly, deeply and wildly in love. She enjoys watching the characters in her books go crazy for each other, but hates to see the blissful couple disappear when it's time for them to live happily ever after. In addition to writing romance novels, Kate also writes fiction and nonfiction for young adults. She lives on Long Island, New York, with her husband and daughter.

For Rosie, the greatest dog you could ever imagine.
Her pure heart and gentle spirit
gave so much love during her brief life.
She will always live on in our hearts.

One

The morning had been absolutely exasperating—even for a Monday, Meredith reflected. She'd missed the bus and gotten caught in a downpour without an umbrella. Not to mention a run in her panty hose that was now as wide as the mighty Mississippi.

She scurried from the elevator to her office at Colette, Inc., the world-renowned jewelry company. She opened the door and slipped inside. Usually a little rain or a ruined stocking wouldn't phase her. Her appearance was always neat and carefully planned to blend into the woodwork. But this morning she had to give a presentation to just about every high-level person in the company. Meredith dreaded speaking to groups, or any situation that put her in the limelight. Having her hair and outfit wrecked by the rain made the job even worse.

With her office door firmly closed behind her, she worked on some basic repairs, starting with her long reddish-brown hair. Matted and damp, it curled in every direction at once. She brushed it back tightly, in her usual style—a simple low ponytail secured with a clip. A bit severe perhaps, but certainly practical. Her complexion was fair, with faint freckles on her nose. She rarely tried to cover them with makeup. In fact, she usually wore no makeup at all. Which was just as well, she thought, since this morning she'd definitely have a bad case of raccoon eyes from melted mascara.

Her large blue eyes stared back at her in the mirror from behind oversize, tortoiseshell frames. She removed the glasses and wiped the damp lenses with a tissue. She often wished she could wear contact lenses and had several pairs in her medicine chest. But her eyes never felt totally comfortable in contacts, especially during the close work required for jewelry design. Besides, she had no one special to impress.

A long floral skirt hid most of the run in her hose, she noticed. But her V-neck sweater, usually so baggy and figure concealing, now clung damply to her body like a second skin. Her mother had often told her that her ample curves on top were a blessing, but Meredith had never felt that way. To the contrary, she felt quite self-conscious about her busty physique and the unwanted attention it brought her, especially from men. Unlike most women she knew, Meredith did all she could to hide her curves, rather than show them off.

The large brooch pinned to her sweater pulled on the wet fabric, and Meredith carefully unfastened the clasp. She took a moment to study the pin, holding it carefully in the palm of her hand. It was amazingly unique. Anyone would notice that. As she was a jewelry designer, it seemed even more remarkable to her. It was a one-of-a-kind item you might come upon in an "arty" shop of handmade jewelry or in a place that handled estate sales and antique pieces. Meredith's landlady, Rose Carson, had given it to her just last night, when she'd been down at Rose's apartment having coffee. Rose was wearing the pin and Meredith had admired it. Then, without any warning at all, Rose took the pin off and offered it to her, insisting that Meredith borrow it for a while.

"Rose, it's lovely. But it must be very precious to you…. What if I lose it?" Meredith had asked.

"Don't be silly, you won't lose it," Rose had insisted. "Here, put it on." Rose had helped Meredith with the clasp. "Let's see how it looks."

Meredith had to agree it looked stunning. Yet, she still felt uncomfortable borrowing such a valuable piece of jewelry. But Rose, in her gracious, gentle way, wouldn't take no for an answer.

The design was roughly circular, a hand-worked base of different precious metals, studded with chunks of amber and polished gemstones. Staring down at it now in her hand, Meredith still found the composition fascinating, almost magically mesmerizing if one stared at it long enough, with the interplay of glittering jewels of so many different colors, shapes and cuts. The flickering shards of light thrown off from the jewels made Meredith feel almost light-headed and she had to look away to regain her bearings. She had the oddest feeling each time she studied the pin, she noticed. But couldn't quite understand why.

Brushing the question aside, she slipped the pin into the deep pocket of her skirt, feeling sure it would be safe there. Rose claimed the pin always brought her luck, and Meredith hoped that it would work for her today at her presentation, even hidden away in her pocket.

At work, she always wore a long gray smock over her

clothing. It protected her clothes while she worked, constructing samples of her jewelry designs, and conveniently for the modest Meredith, also hid her body. She took it down now from the hook behind her door. The smock was a must today, even for the meeting. Without it, I'd look like a contestant in a wet T-shirt contest, she reflected wryly as she fastened the snaps.

Meredith knew she wasn't a "babe"—not like some of the women around the office. She was definitely the type men called a "plain Jane." It had always been that way for her and she doubted now it would ever change. Some women were just born that way. They either had it—or they didn't. Hadn't her glamorous mother always told her so, in one subtle way or another? If she looked a little disheveled today, nobody would care. Nobody would notice.

Meredith took a seat at her drawing table and turned her thoughts to more important matters. She flipped the lid off a paper cup of coffee and took out a large project folder. The folder held the sketches for a new line of wedding bands, her current design project. She removed the sketches and spread them out on her drawing table. It was the line she was due to present at eleven o'clock and she still wanted to do some finishing touches. Her co-workers called her a perfectionist, but Meredith had always thought that the real impact of any piece was always in the details. Since it was so difficult for her to speak at meetings, she needed to walk into a presentation feeling that her work was flawless, otherwise her shyness would get the best of her.

As Meredith reviewed the sketches, she felt pleased. She was proud of the "Everlasting Collection" and eager to see what others thought. The his-and-her wedding rings had been solely her idea, and the simple but elegant designs bore her distinctive, contemporary flair. Yet, part of her found it ironic that she was so adept at creating such perfectly stunning wedding rings, when it seemed so unlikely that a man she loved—a faceless stranger so far—would ever slip a gold band on her finger and pledge his everlasting devotion. Her single attempt at romance during her senior year at college had been a total disaster. One that Meredith believed she'd barely survived. If that's what they called taking a chance on love, Meredith knew she wasn't fit for the game.

Designing wedding rings or heart-shaped lockets or any of the many trinkets lovers exchanged always left her with a feeling that was bittersweet at best. But she would try to distance herself, to tell herself it was her work and there was no need to get emotional. Then she'd go home, put on her grungiest clothes and head out to her studio. Alone in the empty warehouse space, she'd fire up her blowtorch and fuel all her loneliness and frustration into her artwork—her wild-looking abstract metal sculptures.

Sometimes it was hard for Meredith to believe that she had been working at Colette for four years. Time had passed so quickly. It had been her first job out of college, and though she hadn't expected to stay this long, she'd already had two promotions and had never once considered looking for work elsewhere, though a few rival firms had tried to recruit her.

She liked the atmosphere here, the way that everyone worked together without a lot of petty rivalry and office politics which she knew went on in other firms. Over the years, she'd made some very good friends within the company, Jayne Pembroke, Lila Maxwell and Sylvie Bennett, to name her three closest pals, who also happened to live in the same apartment building as she did, on Amber Court.

But how long would she—or anyone else on the payroll—be employed by Colette, Inc.? Rumors of a corporate takeover had started as a vague whisper among the rank and file but now ran rampant through the company. Some hotshot financer named Marcus Grey was buying up as much stock as he could get his hands on. The firm's mysterious predator was moving in for the kill, like a lone wolf poised to strike. The giant jewelry manufacturer had few resources to defend itself. It was now just a waiting game, and morale around the office was at an all-time low.

But like many other employees, Meredith was determined to carry on with an optimistic attitude. That was partly why she was so particular about her work these days. Instead of giving a halfhearted effort, as if the assignments didn't matter anymore, she pushed herself to give her all, to produce designs that were truly inspired and would remind her co-workers that the company did indeed have a future. And everything might just turn out all right in the end.

She gazed down at the second set of sketches and lifted her pencil to add an extra embellishment. The phone rang just as her pencil point hovered above the drawing.

"Meredith Blair," she answered in a businesslike tone.

"It's me," Jayne Randolph answered in a hushed but urgent tone. "You're needed down in the showroom for a consultation."

"The showroom? Do I have to?" Meredith knew she sounded like a five-year-old. But she couldn't help it.

Besides, Jayne was a friend. Surely she'd let her off the hook.

"In a word, yes," Jayne replied.

"Oh, drat."

Meredith hated visiting the showroom. She knew she'd rather starve than have a job in sales, catering to the representatives of large accounts and an upmarket, private clientele. Yet, from time to time designers had to go down for consultations with the sales personnel and a client.

A visit to the showroom usually meant that some spoiled, wealthy woman couldn't find the diamond ring or jewel-studded necklace she had in mind, and now wanted to drive somebody crazy as she tried to describe her jewelry fantasy. Meredith knew that nine times out of ten trying to get it right was an exercise in futility. She doubted that even a mind reader would manage to satisfy such clients. Meredith was much more comfortable hiding away in her studio then being thrust into the limelight.

Besides, if she went down now, she'd never get through the sketches in time. "Come on, Jayne. Can't you call someone else? I'm really absolutely swamped. I'm due to show designs at a big marketing meeting this morning and I'm still cleaning up some rough spots. Can't Anita or Peter help you?"

"I called Frank first," Jayne said. "When I told your boss who the client was, he said to call you. Specifically, *you*, Meredith."

"Who's the client?"

"Adam Richards," Jayne replied solemnly. She spoke in a whisper, so Meredith guessed that Mr. Richards—whoever he was—stood within earshot.

"Am I supposed to know who that is?" she asked, laughing despite herself.

"No offense, Meredith but...what planet do you live on?" Jayne asked sweetly. "Adam Richards? Owns Richards Home Furnishings? One of the company's top private clients? Spends *loads* of money here every year? Just your average, self-made millionaire," she added.

"Oh, *that* Adam Richards," Meredith said lightly. "I find it hard to keep up with the self-made millionaire list lately.... What's he doing now?"

"Pacing around the showroom. In an irritated tycoon sort of way. He's chosen a few items he likes, and he wants to speak to a designer about customizing the designs. I'm going to bring him into room number three and serve him coffee. You'd better get down here right away. I think he knows Frank personally," she added.

Meredith had always gotten along well with her boss. He had taught her so much and encouraged her own creative talents to blossom. But Frank Reynolds still didn't cut any slack for her, though she was probably his favorite. If Frank said she had to go, she had to go.

"All right," Meredith conceded with a sigh. "Tell your average, impatient tycoon I'm on my way."

Meredith hung up the phone, then grabbed her smaller sketchpad and her coffee. As she headed for the door, she thought to check her appearance, maybe swipe on a bit of lip gloss or check her hair again. But then she shrugged off the impulse. Big deal. Adam Richards. So the man had money—a great deal of money. Material success had never impressed her, and she rather disliked people who believed they were due special treatment just because they were wealthy.

She'd be courteous and professional, of course. With any luck, she'd get rid of Mr. Imperious Millionaire quickly and still have some time to review her presentation.

The elevator to the ground floor left her at the end of the long corridor that ran behind the showroom. Meredith soon caught sight of Adam Richards in room number three. He stood with his back turned toward the doorway. The first thing she noticed about him was his broad shoulders and lean build, covered by a charcoal-gray suit. An extremely well-tailored suit, she noticed, which covered his athletic build without a single gap or wrinkle.

He was also quite tall, an inch or so above six feet, she guessed. Meredith always noticed a man's height, since at five-ten in her stocking feet, she was well above average for a woman. She didn't often meet men she could look up to, but here was one. Literally speaking, at least, she thought with a secret smile.

As she drew closer to the doorway, she felt her chronic shyness move over her like a soft, heavy blanket. A smothering cloud. She took a deep breath and willed herself to go forward, to act the part of an efficient, able employee. Wisps of her wavy, reddish-brown hair had come loose from her clip and softly curled around her face. She tried to smooth back the tendrils with her hands, but to no effect.

The sooner started, the sooner done, Meredith reminded herself. Her head down, her sketch book clutched under her arm, she strode purposefully into the room…and nearly walked right into him.

He turned when she entered and quickly stepped to the side. He stared down at her with a dark, steady gaze, apparently startled by her clumsy entrance. He had brown eyes, a rich coffee color, greeting her with a mixture of warmth and curiosity. Meredith met his gaze briefly, then shyly looked away. She could feel her pulse race and her cheeks grow warm.

He was younger than she'd expected. Maybe around forty, she guessed. Weren't self-made tycoons older than that? Older…and balding and paunchy…and far less attractive?

Finally she looked up again. He was still staring down at her, watching her in a way that made her feel even more self-conscious.

"Mr. Richards." She thrust out her hand. "How do you do? I'm Meredith Blair, one of the designers here."

"One of the best, I hear." He took her hand in his larger one and briefly shook it. His grasp was firm and warm. His voice was deep. Deep and definite. The compliment made her blush again, but she tried to ignore it. "Thank you for coming down to see me. I realize now I should have made an appointment. I hope you weren't called away from anything important?"

"No, not at all," Meredith wasn't deceptive by nature, but the little white lie seemed necessary under the circumstances. As in, "The customer is always right." Especially *this* customer.

"Please have a seat, Mr. Richards." She gestured for him to take the chair opposite hers at the small table in the center of the room.

"Please call me Adam," he suggested with a smile. He had even white teeth and deep dimples creased his lean cheeks. The change in his expression, the small lines that crinkled at his eyes and etched his wide, supple mouth made something within her tingle with awareness.

Awareness…and alarm.

He was either a very nice guy, she decided, or so phony, he was able to fake it flawlessly. Meredith knew she was suspicious of men and their motives. Especially good-looking, older men. But she couldn't help it. Experience had been a cruel but able teacher.

She took a moment to arrange the objects on the table. A necessary task that gave her a moment to collect herself. The table was set up for viewing jewelry and had a dark-blue velvet mat in its center. A magnifying lens and a high-intensity lamp with a long bendable neck stood to one side.

She rearranged the lens and lamp to her liking, then pushed up her glasses, which had slid down her nose a bit. Her hands felt strangely shaky, and she hoped he didn't notice.

"I'll try to be brief and not take up too much of your time, Ms. Blair," he began. "Here's the problem. I'd like to give some gifts to my employees at a company banquet that's coming up in a month or two. It's part of our national sales conference, and about five hundred employees usually attend," he explained. "A few retirements will be announced, and the firm always gives an engraved desk clock. But I'd like to give something different this year. A stickpin, perhaps. Or a gold key chain with some sort of medallion or inscription," he suggested. "Then there are awards for outstanding achievement. Especially in the sales force. The employees are receiving a bonus, of course. But I'd like to give them a gift, as well. I'll need about one hundred items in all. Do you think they can be ready by say…the first week in December?"

Meredith watched his face as he spoke. He had a very expressive face, she thought. Her artist's eye appreciated his broad, smooth forehead, the strong lines of his cheeks and jaw, his wide, supple mouth. She thought she would like to do a sketch of him sometime. She also liked the way he looked right into her eyes, meeting her own in such a direct, unguarded manner.

But once he had finished and his gaze remained fixed on hers, she realized that she'd been so distracted, studying him, she'd barely heard a word he'd said.

"The first week in December?" she echoed vaguely.

"Not enough time, you think?" He shook his head. "I always leave these things to the last minute," he admitted. She was surprised at his tone, which was almost...apologetic.

Weren't these rich guys supposed to be much more irate and demanding? Wasn't he supposed to pound his fist on the table or stamp his foot or something?

"Probably. I mean, maybe. I mean, it depends on what you want, specifically, of course," she stammered, staring down at her notepad. "I do know that we'll try to do our best to meet your schedule, Mr. Richards."

She quickly raised her eyes to his and saw that he was grinning. Laughing at her babbling. Oh, Lord. She sounded like an idiot. And felt like one, too.

"It's Adam," he reminded her. "May I call you Meredith?"

She nodded, feeling a lump in her throat the size of a large jelly doughnut. She didn't know what was happening to her. Meredith was typically nervous meeting new people—especially men—but she was usually able to hide it much better. This man was really getting under her skin for some reason, and she willed herself to get a grip on her frazzled nerves. And runaway pulse.

"You're right. I haven't been very specific, have I?" he said, obviously trying to put her at ease. "I found a few things I liked in the display area. I believe Ms. Randolph left them here on the table so that we could discuss them."

"Yes, of course. That will give us a start." Meredith picked up a dark-blue velvet bag that was sitting in front of her on the table and hurriedly opened it.

"Let's see, what do we have here—" she murmured. She withdrew the various items one by one and laid them out on the velvet cushion. As she moved into her working mode, Meredith felt herself relax a bit. It was easier for her to deal with clients once she had something tangible to focus on and could begin the design process.

She picked up the first piece, a 14K yellow-gold stick-pin with an engraved shaft, topped by a square-cut emerald of about one-third a carat in size. The stone was held in a crown-shaped setting, which Meredith didn't care for at all.

"What do you think?" he asked.

She glanced up at him, unsure of whether or not to be frank. She didn't want to insult his taste. On the other hand he had requested her opinion.

"Honestly?" she asked.

"Of course." He sat back in his chair.

"I like the detail on the shaft," she said, turning the piece under the magnifying lens for him to see. "But I don't care much for the setting. It's very ordinary. And a bit…gaudy."

"My feeling exactly." He nodded in perfect agreement, then waited for her to continue, giving her his complete and utmost attention.

Meredith felt better. She had a strong feeling that Adam Richards had good taste. Similar taste to her own, in fact, which would make things a lot easier.

"Most people would wear a small piece like this as an accent to other jewelry," she continued. "A simple, sleeker setting would display the stone more dramatically. And also, be less likely to clash with other items."

She turned the pin over again in her hand, then took it out from under the magnifying glass, set it on the velvet display cushion and looked at it for a few moments.

"Wait...I have an idea." She quickly rose from her seat. "Let's see what you think of this...."

She walked to a polished wood cabinet, withdrew a ring of keys from under her smock and opened the brass lock. She opened the doors to reveal three rows of narrow drawers, like the drawers one might find in an old-fashioned hardware store. Only these drawers held precious stones of various sizes and hues, not screws and washers.

It took her only a few moments to find what she was looking for, and she withdrew several small plastic bags that held gemstones and brought them to the table.

"I want to show you these stones," Meredith said, feeling excited at her inspiration. "They're called cabochons. Perhaps you've seen them before?"

"No...I haven't," Adam replied as he watched her shake out the gems onto the velvet pillow.

"These are uncut gems, polished with an opaque look. I've picked out some sapphires. But all types of colored gems are available as cabochons. Rubies, emeralds, amethyst. Here, take a look," she said, swinging the magnifying lens in his direction.

He peered down at the gems, studying them...and she took a moment to study him. His hair was dark and thick, with a slight wave. Cut conservatively short, he combed it back and to one side, though a thick lock occasionally fell down across his forehead. With the bright light nearby, she noticed how his dark mane was shot through with strands of silver. His face looked intense as he examined the stones, his thick brows drawn together over lean cheeks and square jaw. His chin held a small dimple, that seemed just right. A perfect balance to his long, straight nose.

He was handsome, she thought. Extremely handsome. Though not in the typical way at all. More of a rough-around-the-edges, self-made man way, she silently noted with a small smile at her own private joke. She wondered vaguely why Jayne hadn't warned her about his looks. But then again, Jayne knew very well that any mention of such a thing would have rattled Meredith totally, and made her find some excuse to avoid the meeting altogether.

Adam suddenly looked up. He caught her looking at him, and she felt self-conscious, as if, gazing into her eyes, he had read her thoughts. A slow, knowing smile formed on his supple lips. She felt herself blush and looked back down at the gemstones.

"So...what do you think?" She tried her best to sound casual and professional, but her voice sounded forced and breathless. Just to give herself something to do, she removed her glasses and wiped the lenses on the edge of her smock. It was a nervous habit she had and one she wasn't even conscious of performing.

That is, not until she noticed a strange expression on Adam Richard's face as he stared at her across the narrow table.

"Beautiful," he replied, his tone mindful, appreciative and even surprised. "Absolutely. Very subtle and natural. Very...unconventional."

His quiet words and intense gaze were totally unnerving. Meredith was annoyed with herself and couldn't understand her reaction. It was almost as if, at that moment, he wasn't talking about the gems at all...but describing *her*.

But that was ridiculous. Utterly...insane. She shoved her glasses back on and turned her attention back to the jewelry.

"Uh...good. I'm glad you like them. Let's try one with the pin." She pulled open the small drawer on her side of the table and removed some tools and a vial of setting-glue solvent.

Moments later she'd removed the emerald from the stickpin setting and replaced it with a small sapphire cabochon.

She held it out for Adam's inspection. "What do you think?"

"That's lovely. Perfect," he exclaimed in his quiet, thoughtful way. "May I see it under the lens?"

Then, without waiting for Meredith to hand him the stickpin, he reached out, cupped her hand in his own and moved it beneath the magnifier. His touch felt gentle but firm. She felt as if a sudden shock of electricity coursed up her arm, spreading swiftly through every inch of her body. But Meredith willed herself to remain stone still, not moving a muscle. Barely breathing.

"Yes, it's just right. The sapphire is a good choice, too," he commented, still holding her hand and staring down at the pin. "Though I think I'd like to see others made up with a ruby and an emerald, just to compare. Once we've agreed on the new setting design."

He took his hand away and Meredith placed the stick-pin on the velvet mat. Looking down, she flipped open her notebook, taking a moment to gather her scattered thoughts.

"Yes, of course. A ruby and emerald," she said aloud as she jotted the note in her book. "Here's a rough idea of a new setting design," she added. With a few deft strokes of her pencil she sketched a new design for the pin—a smooth, organic-looking shape with a setting that would wrap around the stone, like green petals of a bud about to unfold.

Adam sat quietly, watching her draw. As she shifted the pad for him to view the sketch, he bent his dark head toward her. The expression on his face told her that he was impressed by her artistic ability. It surprised her somehow. She didn't think a man who had spent his life in such a corporate, commercial atmosphere would recognize or value artistic talent.

Adam Richards certainly wasn't what she had expected. Not at all.

"This is excellent, Meredith." He looked up and met her gaze. "It's just the type of thing I was hoping to find...but couldn't quite put into words," he added with an attractive, appreciative smile that set Meredith's nerve endings tingling. "Could you make a sample for me to see?"

"Of course," she said agreeably.

She was suddenly highly aware of their close proximity, his face just inches from her own as they both remained leaning over the sketch. She blinked and quickly sat bolt upright.

"I could have that ready for you tomorrow afternoon," she said. She swallowed hard and pushed her glasses up higher on her nose.

"That quickly? That's great. Let me check my schedule for tomorrow and see if I'm free..." He withdrew a small black book from the pocket in his suit jacket and flipped it open.

"You don't need to come back here. I mean, I know how busy you must be. We'd be happy to send the piece to your office by messenger," Meredith explained. "Then you can call and let me know what you think."

Was she stuttering? The idea of enduring another one-on-one interview with Adam Richards had her nerves in an uproar all over again. She took a deep breath, hoping he'd agree to her suggestion.

"It's no problem. This time of year is relatively slow for me," he replied lightly, and she had a sinking feeling in her stomach. "Besides, there's more than the stickpin to figure out," he reminded her. "And I'm due back at the office in a few minutes." He glanced briefly at his watch. "Shall we figure out some meeting time for tomorrow?"

"Yes, of course," Meredith replied numbly. She looked down at the table, her lips twisting in a resigned expression. She'd make up the stickpin for him. That would be fun. But as for working with him further...the very thought totally unhinged her. And she didn't want to figure out why.

"What about lunch?" he asked.

Her head snapped up. "Lunch?"

He laughed. "You know, that meal between breakfast and dinner? Don't you eat lunch...or are you one of those women who are forever starving themselves?"

"I'm never on a diet," Meredith replied honestly.

There were times in her life—particularly her adolescence—when Meredith bemoaned her figure. But with the passing years any excess weight had simply melted off her long-limbed frame. Although in her mind she still carried the poor body image of her childhood, in actuality she was slim and fit, practically model-like in proportions. She did nothing extra to stay in shape, getting most of her exercise with long walks or a jog through the park with her Labrador retriever, Lucy. The heavy work required for her metal sculptures also kept her muscles hard. She didn't like most sports, and working out in a gym, in front of all of those mirrors, not to mention the other members, was her idea of damnation. As for dieting, she wasn't a junk-food junky, but loved to eat and rarely deprived herself.

"Never on a diet, eh? How refreshing," Adam replied brightly. "So I can take you someplace tomorrow where they serve real food, instead of rabbit feed?" he persisted. "I know just the place. How about Crystal's?"

Crystal's? That was the most exclusive restaurant in Youngsville, Indiana. She'd never been there, but had heard one needed to wait a month for a reservation. Of course, not if you were a regular, as Adam Richards no doubt was.

"I've heard it's lovely. Thanks for the invitation...but I don't think I can have lunch with you," Meredith stammered. She rose from her seat and hurriedly gathered her pad and coffee.

"Oh, why not? I think we can get a lot done over lunch," Adam persisted. He rose, as well, and stood in front of her, blocking her escape route from the small room. He stood so close that when she looked up to answer him, she had to tilt her head back.

"Yes, I'm sure we'd get work done," she said diplomatically, remembering that he was, after all, an important client. "But I believe I'll be in a meeting that will be going on all afternoon."

That was a lie. There was no meeting. But she didn't know what else to say.

"How about Wednesday, then? Do you have a meeting on Wednesday?" he asked. His voice was soft, with a faint note of amusement, she thought. He had guessed she was lying to him. Still, she couldn't understand why he was so insistent about taking her out to lunch.

"I...I have to check. I'm not sure." Meredith hugged

her sketchbook to her chest and decided to charge for the door. ‘‘I’ll call your office and let you know.’’

‘‘All right.’’ He nodded and smiled slightly, trying to suppress a huge grin, she guessed. He was laughing at her. Finding it terribly amusing that a woman would be so flustered by a simple invitation to lunch. She felt silly…but couldn’t help it.

She looked down, avoiding his gaze as she moved toward the doorway. She just wanted to leave, to get away from him and be alone. But then she did something even more stupid. In her rush to flee she spilled coffee on herself. She felt the warm liquid seep through her smock and sweater. She looked down and saw what had happened.

‘‘Oh…darn,’’ she muttered aloud. She dropped her pad to the floor and placed the leaky cup on the table. With her arms sticking out on either side, she looked down to survey the damage. Her gray smock was dripping with coffee, a huge stain spreading on one side. She couldn’t bear to see what had happened to her pale sweater and skirt.

‘‘Here, let me get that for you,’’ Adam said as he quickly bent to retrieve her pad. ‘‘I’m so sorry…did I bump into you or something?’’ he asked with genuine concern.

‘‘No…not at all. I manage to create these little disasters all on my own,’’ Meredith explained. She still stood with her arms at her side, coffee now dripping from her smock to the floor.

‘‘But I was standing in your way. You couldn’t get by,’’ he said, making an excuse for her. ‘‘Can I help you get that off?’’ Adam asked politely.

‘‘Uh, no…I can manage, thanks.’’

The moment of truth had arrived. She had to take the smock off, it was dripping on her shoes.

She carefully undid the snaps, then slipped it off her shoulders and rolled it in a ball to contain the wet spot. Her sweater, still damp from her soaking in the rain, clung to her like a second skin. It now had an ugly brown stain covering a large portion of the pale fabric. A hopeless kind of stain that would probably never come out, she guessed.

"Oh, well. Guess I need to go find another smock," she said, trying to sound offhand about the fumble.

She looked up at Adam and saw a strange light in his eyes. A totally masculine glow that scared her to death. He hadn't been staring at the coffee stain all this time...but studying her figure. She was sure of it. She was just as sure that he'd never expected that beneath her baggy gray camouflage there was anything worth looking at.

She thought she had long ago outgrown self-consciousness about her hourglass proportions. At that moment, however, it didn't seem so. At least he didn't ogle her, but quickly looked away, his expression once again returning to a friendly smile.

"Well...here's your pad." Now it was his turn to seem self-conscious and momentarily off balance as he handed her the sketchpad. "And take my card," he added, handing her a business card. "On second thought, I'll have my secretary call you later to set up another appointment."

"That sounds fine," Meredith said, backing toward the door. She held the sketchpad to her chest, though it offered little coverage. His secretary. Good. She wouldn't have to make excuses to him. It would be even easier that way.

"Well, so long, Meredith. Thanks for your help," he said as she left the room. "I look forward to seeing the stickpin."

"I'll have it made up for you soon, Mr. Richards.... And, you're very welcome," she added, remembering her manners. She also remembered that she was supposed to call him by his first name. But she didn't want to. She needed to put some distance between them now, to put things back on a more businesslike level. She had finally reached the door and quickly turned and opened it.

"Goodbye, now," she called over her shoulder as she left him.

"Goodbye, Meredith," he returned. "See you soon."

His soft, deep voice did not sound businesslike, or impersonal at all, she noticed as she raced away toward the elevator.

Two

Feeling totally rattled, Meredith hurried down the hall to her office, grabbed a clean smock from the closet and gathered up the sketches that were still spread across her drawing table. It was five to eleven and she had no time to review the drawings any further. At least she wouldn't be late for the meeting, she thought as she dashed out of her office and headed for the large conference room at the end of the corridor.

Despite her unsettling interview with Adam Richards, Meredith managed to collect herself enough to give her presentation. As she took her seat, she could not recall a word she had said. It had all gone by in a nervous blur. Her friends, Sylvie and Lila, who both worked in the marketing department, were present and kept shooting Meredith encouraging smiles. She was sure they'd each drop by her office later to review her performance.

Judging from the reactions of the rest of her colleagues—especially the pleased expression on her supervisor's face—Meredith knew she must have done well. Even the crankiest sales manager seemed excited by the new line. Meredith listened to the comments and noted the various suggestions made, all the while quietly swelling with pride.

Buoyed by her success, she returned to her office and ate lunch at her desk as she worked through the afternoon. The embarrassing moment with Adam Richards didn't seem nearly as awful now. Meredith could practically laugh at herself...if it wasn't for the ruined sweater.

Meredith had just finished her lunch when Lila called. Lila said she thought Meredith had done a terrific job at the meeting and that she absolutely loved the new designs.

"Nick was very impressed," she added, mentioning her boss, who was the Vice President of Overseas Marketing and also happened to be Lila's fiancé. "I hope the company puts them into production soon," she added. "I'd love to have a set of the bands in time for our wedding."

Lila and Nick hadn't set a wedding date yet, but Meredith knew that they were so crazy about each other, it was going to be a very short engagement.

"Don't worry, Lila. I can always make a set for you," Meredith promised, "even if the company decides not to use the collection."

Or, if Marcus Grey succeeds in buying out Colette and shutting us down, she nearly added. But she didn't want to voice the gloomy possibilities, especially on such an upbeat day.

After she finished her call with Lila, Meredith realized that she'd never received a call from Adam's secretary.

She was surprised. He'd seemed so adamant about pinning her down for another appointment. His business card sat on her drawing table, tucked under a clip. She glanced at it but didn't even dare think of calling his office. Perhaps he was the type of guy who seemed all excited at the moment about something…then, minutes later, was on to something else.

Oh, well, so much the better. Maybe he'd forget all about his custom-designed trinkets and decide to give out monogrammed umbrellas or tote bags. Maybe she'd never hear from him again.

The idea should have been heartening, but somehow didn't sit well with her. Then Meredith's musings were interrupted by a knock on her partially opened door.

Meredith turned in her seat to see Sylvie in the doorway. Sylvie usually visited her at work at least once a day, to chat and catch up. They also saw each other at home, since Sylvie was Meredith's neighbor.

After they met, they realized they had many things in common. Though they both had a tendency to be loners, over recent months they'd become close friends. Like Meredith, Sylvie rarely dated and also looked back on her upbringing with mixed emotions. But, Meredith often reflected, unlike Sylvie, at least she'd been raised by two parents who loved her. Even if they didn't love each other. Orphaned as an infant, Sylvie had no family and had been raised in foster homes. She'd left the system when she was eighteen and eventually came to work for Colette, Inc., where she was presently the assistant director of marketing. While such a childhood would have made many people bitter, Sylvie was just the opposite. Her bright, warm, upbeat personality easily won her friends and cheered everyone who knew her. She looked upon the company as her family, and it seemed that her co-workers loved her in the same way.

Everybody loved Sylvie...and loved to confide in her. Sylvie just had a way of finding out the juiciest company gossip. As Sylvie took a seat, Meredith was sure her friend had come to deliver the news about the takeover.

"You really wowed them this morning. Marianne already called a meeting about the ad campaign," Sylvie reported, mentioning one of the marketing managers. "A full-page ad in a leading bridal magazine, for starters."

Meredith usually met such news calmly, but even she was excited to hear that her designs were so successful. "Really? I didn't even start the samples yet," she mused aloud.

"Sounds like you'd better. What are you working on now?"

Sylvie peered over Meredith's shoulder at the stickpin Meredith had designed for Adam Richards. Meredith had worked on it most of the afternoon and it was almost done. She felt the urge to confide totally in Sylvie about her meeting with the handsome, seemingly single, self-made millionaire, but suddenly stopped herself. She didn't want to talk about him. Not even to Sylvie. She felt a giant lump in her throat even thinking about him. She was acting like a teenager.

She pushed the stickpin aside and turned back to her friend. "It's nothing. Just a sample I need to put together for a client. Any news about the takeover?" she asked, hoping to change the subject.

"No really big news." Sylvie shrugged and pushed back a lock of her shiny black hair. Meredith had often noticed her friend's beautiful hair, a perfect match to Sylvie's warm-brown eyes. "I think Grey has picked up a few more shares of stock, but he still has a way to go before he holds fifty-one percent.'' Sylvie's eyes darkened as she spoke about the company's adversary and Meredith could practically feel her friend's righteous indignation. ''The word is that once he gains control of the company, he plans to destroy it. He just wants to see Colette wiped out. Nobody really knows why. Somebody has to stop that guy.''

''Yes, of course,'' Meredith agreed with a sigh. ''But who? It would have to be someone with an awful lot of money...or someone who could cause Grey to have a change of heart.''

''If the man even has a heart,'' Sylvie said. ''I just hate to see morale get so low around here. We can't just give up. That's what he wants. We really have to pick up our skirts and plow on.''

Sylvie's folksy, upbeat expression made Meredith laugh.

''Which for some odd reason reminds me, Meredith...you never gave me a firm answer about the auction. You'll do it, won't you? First I lost Jayne, and then Lila,'' she said, mentioning their mutual friends who had both recently become married and engaged. There's a real shortage of gorgeous single females this year and we really need you,'' Sylvie pleaded.

For many years Colette, Inc., had sponsored a bachelorette auction, with all proceeds going to a local orphanage. The same orphanage in fact where Sylvie had lived for many years, so of course the cause was close to her heart and she always took on a large role in the planning. The annual black tie event was very upscale and would be held this year in the ballroom of the city's fanciest hotel, the Fairfield Plaza. The guest list included the most prominent social figures in the city. Meredith always bought a ticket to contribute to the cause. But had never attended. She really disliked large, formal events.

This year, however, not only were her friends pressing her to attend, but they wanted her to step up on the auction block. The very idea made Meredith want to run to the nearest airport and book a one-way ticket to Brazil.

Of course she couldn't do that.

But neither could she dress up in an evening gown, step up on a stage and display herself as strange men made bids to "buy her" for the night. She'd rather be boiled in oil. She'd rather be tarred and feathered. She'd rather be asked to shimmy up a greasy flagpole with a rose in her teeth. She'd rather—

"You're going to do it, right?" Sylvie asked point-blank, interrupting Meredith's thoughts. "I can come over tonight to help you with your outfit. Jayne and Lila said they'd come, too. I'll bring dinner. How about Chinese?"

"Well…tonight's not so good, actually," Meredith fibbed. She tried to meet her friend's steady gaze but couldn't.

"Meredith…I know that look in your eye," Sylvie said, calling her out. "You've got to do it. I won't take no for an answer. We've got to pull together around here. The auction is a chance to show Marcus Grey that we're carrying on, business as usual. We're not rolling over and giving in to him."

While Meredith had to agree with Sylvie's point, she still didn't feel entirely persuaded that if she paraded around a stage in a tight gown and heels—wiggling her extremities for the highest bidder—the effort would do much to thwart the heartless corporate raider.

"Meredith, please. You know how much this means

to me. It's just got to be a good auction this year. The absolute best. We have to show that man what we're made of,'' her friend insisted. ''I know how shy you are and I know this is hard for you. Really, I do. But it might be a good thing for you, too. I mean, you're absolutely gorgeous...but nobody but me and a few other select people even have a chance to realize it. I want everybody in this company to know what a babe you are. They'll be talking about that for months,'' Sylvie added in a teasing tone. ''Won't you help...please?''

Meredith wanted to refuse her...but she couldn't let her friend down. This event was important to Sylvie, and to the entire corporate image. If the charity event went off successfully, as it usually did, it would show a strong united front to Marcus Grey.

And something else in Sylvie's words had rung true. Maybe it was time she stopped hiding like a scared little mouse in a hole, Meredith realized. Maybe forcing herself to get out on that stage would be good for her. If she had a few more ounces of self confidence, maybe she wouldn't act so flustered by a man's mere invitation to lunch. As she had with Adam Richards.

''Okay, you've got me. I'll do it,'' Meredith finally agreed.

''Fantastic!'' Sylvie leaned over and enveloped her in a huge hug. ''I knew you wouldn't let me down. Do you have anything at home you can wear?''

''How about that gray silk dress I wore for the Christmas party?'' Meredith asked.

Sylvie's lovely brow crinkled in a frown. ''I'm not sure I remember.... Oh, yes. The gray silk. It had long sleeves and a sort of high, cowl neck?''

Meredith nodded. Sylvie smiled and shook her head.

"Don't worry, I'll bring over a few things. We'll come up with something great," Sylvie promised.

Meredith was worried. She knew that her idea of "great" and Sylvie's were probably a fashion galaxy apart. But she tamped down her fears and put on a brave smile.

"Chinese sounds good. And don't forget an extra dumpling for Lucy," she added, remembering her dog's favorite treat. "And don't worry, Sylvie. I won't you let you down."

"I know that," Sylvie assured her, and Meredith knew she was telling the truth. Although Meredith didn't make friends easily, her connections were deeply felt. True to her word and loyal to a fault, she'd go the limit to help a friend in need and never went back on her promises.

"Don't worry, this will be fun," Sylvie promised as she rose from her seat. "Oh, I almost forgot..." Sylvie stared down at the package she'd been holding, a medium-size box wrapped in brown paper. "The receptionist asked me to give you this," Sylvie explained. "It was delivered a little while ago."

She glanced at the label as she handed Meredith the box. "Hmm, it's from Chasan's," she noted, naming one of the most expensive clothing stores in town. "I thought you did your shopping at the outlet mall, Meredith. Did you go out on a spree without telling me?"

"I've never been to Chasan's. There must be some mistake." Meredith examined the package and saw her name printed on the label.

Clearly too curious to leave, Sylvie stood by as Meredith tore off the paper and found the trademark, dark-blue gift box tied with a thick gold ribbon. She untied the ribbon and opened the box. Under a layer of gold tissue paper, she found a beautiful pale-pink sweater set, much like the one she had on. However, with one touch, she could tell it was of a far finer quality…and far more expensive than her own.

Meredith took the sweater set out of the paper and Sylvie gasped, "God…that's gorgeous. Who is it from? Is it your birthday or something?"

"My birthday's in June. You know that," Meredith replied, without glancing at her friend. She took a deep breath before reading the gift card she found inside. She already guessed who had sent the gift, but could hardly believe it.

Meredith,

Are you sure I didn't bump into you this morning? You insisted that I didn't, but I still feel responsible somehow for ruining your lovely sweater. Please accept this gift with my appreciation for your help today—and my hope that I'll see you again soon.

Adam

Meredith felt a bit shocked as she placed the card back in the box and closed the lid. It appeared he had picked the sweater set out and bought it himself. Had he really gone to so much trouble for her?

"Who's Adam?" Sylvie asked, and Meredith realized her friend had read the card over her shoulder.

"It's a long story, Sylvie," Meredith replied.

"Judging from that blush on your face, I'll bet it's a good one." Sylvie laughed, her lovely face alight with interest. "You'd better tell all tonight, dear," she warned, "or no fried dumplings."

"In that case, I guess I have to," Meredith replied with a grin. "But there's nothing to tell, honestly. He's just a client, and I'm doing some special designs for him."

"Right, you meet some client this morning and he sends you a hand-delivered gift from Chasan's. But there's *nothing* to tell." Sylvie smiled knowingly and gently patted her friend's shoulder. "Meredith, we need to talk."

"Don't you have enough torture planned for tonight? You don't need to give me a lecture about men, too, Sylvie," she warned in a good-natured tone.

"Me? Give you advice about men? Don't be silly. I'm leaving that job to Lila and Jayne. After all, Jayne's married and Lila's engaged. They both should know something about the species." With a quick wave Sylvie suddenly disappeared through the doorway.

Left alone with her surprise package, Meredith stared down at the box, which sat squarely in her lap. She opened the lid, looked at the sweater set again—now noticing the label of an exclusive European designer—then she looked at the card. She liked his handwriting. It was neat and crisp, with thick, blocky letters. Straightforward as the man himself, she thought.

Oh, dear. She was sinking into some type of warm, romantic mire, like a big steamy bubble bath. Inch by inch, minute by minute. Even though she'd forced Adam Richards's image out of her mind today, she still felt her attraction to him gaining a hold on her.

But she simply wouldn't allow such a thing to happen. She just could not allow it.

Meredith stood and stuck the box in her office closet. She would return the gift to him with a polite, but curt note. She'd complete the sample stickpin, as she had promised; but she would make Frank assign a new designer to the project. She would not permit herself to see Adam Richards again. Certainly not alone. Absolutely not for anything as social as a "fake" business lunch date.

She wasn't as naive about men as her friend Sylvie suspected. She knew what this ride was all about, the uphill climb of the roller coaster car was totally exhilarating—the thrill of a lifetime. It was the downhill slide, and the unavoidable crash, that she feared. Feared with all her heart. Or what was left of it.

Meredith had felt this strongly this quickly about a man only once before. Years ago, in college. Jake was superficially very different from Adam, but in many respects they were much alike, she realized. An established artist, Jake was a visiting professor at her college for a year, and students clamored for the chance to study with him. Jake chose only students he felt were the most promising, and Meredith was thrilled to win a place in his sculpture studio during her senior year. She'd expected to learn a lot about art—not about love. But from the very first moment he spoke to her, other than to critique her work, she felt as if she'd been struck by lightning. She kept her crush a secret from even her closest friends for weeks, never once dreaming her feelings could be returned. But miraculously they were, and she soon entered into a torrid affair with him, agreeing to secrecy in order to keep Jake out of trouble with the school authorities. It was certainly against the school's policy for professors to seduce their students.

He was older, more mature and experienced. A man with status, who could have just about any woman he wanted. He'd swept her off her feet, and the force of his desire had been heady, intoxicating, too much to resist.

But the romance—Meredith's first—had ended badly. Very badly. Meredith was so heartbroken at one point, she didn't get out of bed for weeks. Feeling empty and lost, so worthless and humiliated by Jake's rejection, all she did was cry.

While logically she knew that all men weren't as selfish and heartless as Jake Stark, she simply couldn't risk it. She believed that while other women had some special sense of sniffing out the nice guys from the phonies, she had none. She didn't trust her judgment about men as far as she could toss her living room sofa, and felt far safer not taking any risks.

It took her years to gain her confidence back after Jake, and Meredith knew that in some ways she'd never really recovered. But she finally felt in control of her life and her emotions—happy and productive and standing on steady ground again. Maybe her life wasn't perfect. Maybe she was lonely at times and wished that she had someone close to share her ups and downs. Someone to love wholeheartedly, who loved her in return.

But the risk of failing at that game was too great. The price for losing too high. When she felt blue and needed a lift, she turned to her work at Colette and her sculptures. She turned to her friends, like Sylvie, Jayne, Lila or Rose Carson, her landlady. Or even to her dog, Lucy, who always had a way of bringing a smile to Meredith's gloomiest hours.

The thought of Lucy made Meredith glance at the clock. It was past five, and Lucy was waiting for her walk. Meredith got her work in order, collected her belongings and left her office. She, too, looked forward to the nightly stroll. It gave her a chance to unwind and renew. As she left the office building, she said goodnight to a few friends. Outside, a cool breeze greeted her. The morning's wet weather had cleared and except for some lingering traces of snow on the ground from last month's freak snowstorm, the November evening was dry and the darkening sky, cloudless.

After a short bus ride to her neighborhood, Meredith got off at the Ingalls Park stop and walked across the park to Amber Court. Her apartment building, 20 Amber Court, was a large limestone building, built at the turn of the century. It had once been a private mansion, but was converted into four levels of apartments at some point in the seventies. Meredith loved old houses and had even studied a bit about Victorian architecture. She'd fallen in love with the old building at first sight, and the owner, Rose Carson, who lived on the first floor, had been so warm and welcoming that Meredith had felt right at home from the very first day she'd moved in.

She let herself into the front door and then picked up her mail in the large marble foyer—a magazine, some bills, some junk mail and a letter from her mother.

The sight of her mother's handwriting filled Meredith with mixed emotions. The return address was Malibu Beach in California, where her mother had moved after her parents' divorce, many years ago. Meredith guessed that her mother was writing to invite Meredith to visit for Thanksgiving. The envelope was so thick it might even contain another plane ticket, she speculated. But Meredith didn't want to fly out to the West Coast for the holiday. She would have to make some excuse, of course. She didn't want to think about that problem now, and shoved the letter, along with the rest of the envelopes, into the magazine.

Her apartment was on the third floor. As it was situated at the front of the building, many of the windows afforded a breathtaking view of Ingalls Park. Though the building had a small elevator that had been installed during the renovation, Meredith usually preferred to take the stairs.

Once at her front door, she heard Lucy on the other side, sniffing and whining as Meredith unlocked the door. Meredith had adopted the golden-colored Labrador retriever from a shelter several years ago, and Lucy knew better by now than to jump up. But still, every time Meredith came home, Lucy acted like a puppy and could barely contain her excitement. She ran toward Meredith, carrying a chewed-up tennis ball in her mouth, her tail beating a mile a minute against Meredith's legs. Finally she dropped the ball at Meredith's feet, then licked any part of her owner she could get close to.

''Oh, hello, Lucy. Hello sweetheart,'' Meredith bent to greet her four-legged pal, patting her soft head and rubbing her chest.

''Thank you for the ball, Lucy,'' she crooned, as if the gooey tennis ball was a true treasure. ''Gee, everyone's giving me presents today.''

Lucy sat as still as she could manage in her excited state, content to have the thick, soft fur on her chest rubbed. She leaned forward and covered Meredith's cheek with a sloppy lick.

Meredith laughed and ruffled Lucy's silky ears. ''You're such a sweetheart. I don't know what I'd do without you,'' she said and knew it was true.

Meredith stood up and smoothed out her clothes. ''Go get your leash,'' she told Lucy. ''Let's go out.''

The dog jumped up and darted away, reappearing seconds letter with her thick blue leash in her mouth. Meredith patted her head and clipped on the leash, then allowed Lucy to drag her out of the door and down the stairs as they headed for the park.

The weather was so wonderful that Meredith gave the dog an extra-long walk. She returned home feeling tired but invigorated, as if the cool breeze tossing the treetops in Ingalls Park had somehow blown loose the cobwebs in her mind.

She had just enough time to feed Lucy, then shower and change into comfortable clothes before Sylvie, Lila and Jayne arrived. Her friends bustled in, one carrying a paper bag of Chinese food that emitted warm, appetizing aromas, and the other an armload of evening clothes.

"Here we are," Lila said.

"Right on time," Sylvie added.

Meredith gritted her teeth and grinned. "May the condemned woman at least eat one last meal in peace?"

"Sorry, you'll have to eat while we work on the hair and makeup," Jayne said, glancing at her watch. "I need to get home by nine for Erik."

"These newlyweds," Sylvie rolled her eyes. "Don't worry, I wouldn't dare ask why."

"Don't be silly. He needs some help with his computer," Jayne replied curtly.

"Right," Sylvie said.

Meredith saw Jayne blush scarlet but she made no teasing comment to second Sylvie's. If she were married to Erik, she'd want to get home early, too. Jayne had gone through so much in her life and it was great to know she'd finally found real happiness. Orphaned at age eighteen, she'd given up her own chance to go to college and bravely raised her siblings, who were four years younger. Her younger sister and brother, who were twins, were now away at college. Jayne missed them terribly, but also appreciated the time alone with her new husband.

Lila tried to hide her smile as she turned to open a small overnight case filled with beauty supplies.

"So, are you ready?" Lila asked. She turned to Meredith, brandishing her weapon of choice, a huge, fluffy makeup brush.

"Right," Sylvie said. "So, are you ready?" Sylvie asked turning to Meredith.

"As ready as I'll ever be. Let the games begin...." Meredith said.

Meredith had balked at first at all their fussing, then sat back and allowed herself to enjoy it. Having her friends make her over, from head to toe as shown in the fashion magazines, reminded her of her college days—the best memories of her college days.

She had been a social disaster in high school. A straight-A student and a total bookworm with a few close friends who were equally "geeky."

Her father—a high-powered corporate attorney—was hardly home. When he was, he rarely had time for her. His affection and approval seemed to come in limited doses.

Her mother, a former actress who prided herself on a glamorous image, had tried time and again to make improvements on Meredith's appearance. "You have assets, dear," her mother would assure her. "We just need to bring them out more." Meredith secretly did not see her assets and thought her mother was just trying to be nice. She believed that no amount of new clothes or haircuts would ever make her small-boned and blond like her mother. But trying hard to please her mother—to win the love and approval she'd never truly felt as a child—Meredith wore the fashions or hairstyles her mother advised, feeling silly and uncomfortable most of the time. She squinted and blinked as she forced herself to wear contact lenses. In time she'd finally given up and reverted to her baggy, dull clothes, her dowdy hair-dos and thick lenses. Her mother would rail and moan about the wasted effort, the wasted money—and even call her only child a lost cause. Meredith would burrow even deeper into her shell, hiding her tears behind a favorite novel.

But in college, far from home, Meredith found friends who shared her interests and views, who made her feel valued and appreciated just as she was. She began to develop her own style—a style of dressing and acting that was far different from her conventional, status-conscious parents. Meredith had always known she was different—but for the first time in her life, she began to see that difference as her true asset. An asset she tried to make shine through.

There were some wonderful years in college, and Meredith gained self-confidence and feelings of self-worth. Even her parents noticed the difference when she came home for holiday visits. "A late bloomer," her mother pronounced, and though Meredith could tell she hadn't at all bloomed into the exotic flower her mother had hoped for, Carolyn Blair was nonetheless impressed.

Of course, falling in love with Jake had made her positively glow. There was no lotion or cosmetic in the world that could improve a woman's looks as much as falling in love.

But all that ended just at the time she graduated college. That was when Jake abruptly returned to New York, leaving her a cool, terse note, despite the fact he had promised more than once to take her with him and introduce her to his well-known circle. Why had he treated her so badly? Meredith knew she'd never fully understand it. All she knew was that, along with losing

Jake, she'd lost her special glow. She'd returned home to Chicago defeated and depressed, and reverted to her old dowdy ways of dressing, as if to avoid male attention all together.

It was barely an hour later—though it felt like days to Meredith—when her friends sat back, satisfied with the results of their hard work. Despite Meredith's pleas, they wouldn't allow her to see herself in the mirror until they were completely finished. Probably afraid she'd bolt for the door and escape into the night, she thought.

She could only gather hints about her appearance from their conversation, while they talked about her in the third person, as if she was a mannequin in a store window, all evening long.

"I love her hair that way," Lila said.

"She should wear it like that every day," Jayne insisted.

"That was a total inspiration," Sylvie replied, congratulating Jayne on the hairstyle. "I wasn't thinking up at all, because of the curls. But it looks fantastic like that."

"But you did the makeup. She has such gorgeous blue eyes. I never knew," Jayne said honestly. "It must be the eyebrows."

"That hurt like the dickens," Meredith piped up.

"Come on, Meredith. I only tweezed about three hairs," Lila said. "The eyes were easy. I really like the lips. Put a little lip liner on this woman and she looks like that actress in *Titanic*. What's her name again?"

"Kate Winslet?" Sylvie replied. "I think she looks more like Julia Roberts. Kate Winslet has a round face. This girl's got cheekbones to die for. Not to mention that figure..."

Meredith had heard enough. Even though it was two

of her closest female friends in the world singing her praises, her cheeks were fiery red under all her makeup.

"Look, I appreciate all the compliments, but I don't look a whit like Julia Roberts on her *worst* day...or Kate...whatever her name is, for that matter."

"You're a total knockout, Meredith. Get used to it," Jayne advised blandly.

"You're totally hot, my friend. I think we'd better give you a parasol or something to beat off the men," Sylvie added. "You are going to fetch a high price on Friday night. I bet you'll be the record breaker."

Friday night. A high price. The auction...

In all the fun Meredith had nearly forgotten what this game of dress up was all about. She felt her mouth grow dry and cottony and couldn't answer her friends. Taking a deep breath that threatened to pop the makeshift fastening of her midnight-blue satin evening gown, Meredith felt goose bumps break out on her skin—much of which was exposed by her low neckline.

Could she really, truly do it? The only saving grace would be that in this getup, nobody she worked with would ever recognize her. Maybe she could appear under an assumed name?

"Okay, you're done. You can look now," Lila's voice broke into Meredith's rambling thoughts.

She got up from her seat and walked into her bedroom to view herself in the full-length mirror behind her bedroom door. Her entourage, Sylvie, Lila, Jayne and even Lucy, followed close behind. The four-inch heels, with their sexy thin straps, made every step a shaky challenge, and she stumbled a little on the hardwood floor.

"Don't worry. You'll get used to the heels," Jayne promised her. Meredith doubted she would but didn't say so.

Finally she stood before the mirror. She could hardly believe her eyes and couldn't speak. It was hard to believe that the image she found reflected was indeed her own familiar self. From head to toe, she'd been completely transformed, her thick, reddish-brown hair upswept like a French movie star, with makeup that gave her blue eyes a smoldering look and her wide mouth a sexy red pout. She'd agreed to wear her contact lenses for the event, and Jayne had brought along a new type of solution that made the lenses more comfortable. Even with all the makeup, Meredith found the lenses hardly bothered her tonight at all.

The dress had been a real challenge for her friends, since none of them had Meredith's height or build. They'd finally decided on a midnight-blue satin gown that was so formfitting it appeared to be poured over Meredith's long curvy body. Since it was strapless, it was the only dress that could accommodate Meredith's full proportions on top. *But only because half of me is spilling out,* she now noticed.

"Don't you think the neckline's a little too low?" she asked her friends.

"Not at all," they answered in unison.

"Isn't it too tight in back?" she asked as she checked her rearview.

"That's the style. It's supposed to fit like that," Sylvie assured her.

"Besides, you've got nothing to hide, Meredith," Lila added.

"Well, I couldn't in this outfit," Meredith murmured.

"You look great, Meredith, honestly," Jayne said. "I know the look is a little sexier than you're used to, but everyone's going to be dressed this way. You won't feel out of place at all."

"And remember, it's all for a good cause," Sylvie reminded her. "Oh, I nearly forgot. You need some jewelry. How about these earrings?"

Sylvie handed Meredith a pair of large, pearl drop earrings. Though she rarely wore costume pieces, Meredith agreed that the earrings suited the outfit well. As she clipped them on, she stared at her image in the mirror.

She did look good, she had to admit. Better than good. She looked great...in a fake, glamorous sort of way. She surely wasn't going to dress this way for the rest of her life, but it was fun for once. Like putting on a costume or taking on a role in a play.

"It's just like Cinderella," Sylvie piped up. Then, glancing at Meredith's expression, she added, "Oh, no offense, Meredith. I didn't mean it in a bad way."

"I know," Meredith said with a smile. "It is like Cinderella...if her fairy godmother shopped at Victoria's Secret."

"Cute. Now all we need is a mail-order prince," Jayne said.

Meredith suddenly thought of Adam Richards. Then felt angry at herself. But it would be something if he could see her dressed like this, she thought. A far cry from her coffee-soaked exit. Then she felt terrified at the realization he might actually be attending the affair. She had to find out from Sylvie if he'd be there. Sylvie was organizing the event and would certainly have access to the guest lists.

She wouldn't ask now, though, Meredith decided. She'd just make her friends curious and then be answering a lot of questions.

"Well, are we done now? Can I change back into my sweatpants?" Meredith asked.

"I wish Rose could see you," Lila said. "Can I call her?"

Over the years they had all grown close to Rose Carson, each in their way. She'd been like a mother to each of them, and they loved her dearly. Rose was the one person Meredith would allow to see her dressed in this vixen look.

"Oh, yes. Let's call her," Meredith turned, and picked up the phone.

"Oh, wait, I think she's out tonight," Jayne said. "She works at the shelter on Monday now."

"That's right. I forgot," Meredith replied as she replaced the phone. Rose was very active in the community and worked two nights a week at a local homeless shelter and soup kitchen. She rarely came home by ten, and the time was just approaching nine.

"She's coming to the auction," Sylvie said. "In fact, I think I'm going to assign her the very important job of escorting you over, so you don't chicken out."

"Who, me? Chicken out?" Meredith asked innocently. "Don't be silly."

She struggled to open the top of the gown, and Sylvie came around to help her. "No comment," Sylvie replied. "All you have to do is put on the dress and earrings. I'll do your hair and makeup backstage."

A short time later her friends packed up and left for home. Lila went down the hall. Sylvie headed for her apartment upstairs, on the fourth floor, and Jayne for the new home she now shared with Erik only a few blocks away. After her friends left, she took Lucy out for a quick walk, then got ready for bed. She used nearly an entire jar of cold cream and a box of tissues to remove all the makeup, and washing the spray out of her hair in the shower was another challenge. But finally, restored to her old self, Meredith was ready for bed.

As she shut the light and slipped under the covers, she caught sight of the blue satin evening gown, hanging on the outside of her closet door. With the satin heels standing in place on the floor right below, the gown seemed like a ghost of her new, glamorous self. My evil twin, she joked. She blinked to clear the image as she turned off the bedside lamp.

Could she really go through with the auction? she wondered once more. She had promised Sylvie, and now everyone was counting on her. She couldn't let them down.

But what if Adam Richards was there? In that size crowd she could easily avoid him. They wouldn't even have to say hello. But still, she'd rather die than let him see her making such a spectacle of herself, dressed like a sexpot, up on an auction block no less. But now it seemed she really had to go through with it, whether *he* was in the audience or not.

When the hour of truth arrived, Meredith honestly didn't know what she would do. And she only had four short days to figure it out.

Three

The rest of the week passed quickly. The sales and marketing department was very excited about the Everlasting Collection, and Meredith's boss asked her to produce the sample rings by the following week. She had to work late every night to meet the deadline, but she didn't really mind. Crafting pieces of jewelry was always her favorite part of the process and she was very eager herself to see her ideas take form.

The added workload also gave her a convenient excuse to hand off Adam Richards's work to another designer. She completed the sample stickpin she and Adam had discussed, then sent it by messenger to his office, along with the sweater set and a polite but businesslike note. And that was that, she hoped.

She wasn't sure who Frank would assign to Adam's project. There was the new designer, Peter. He was talented but inexperienced. Anita Barnes was the more likely choice. She was quite attractive and single and, as everyone knew, looking to hook a wealthy husband. All told, Anita was much more Adam Richards's speed, Meredith thought. Anita would know how to play up to a man like Adam. She wouldn't be so quick to return expensive gifts, either, Meredith thought.

Meredith didn't know why the image of Adam working with Anita nettled her so much. But it did. And so did the little message slips that she would pick up at the receptionist desk all week long, noting Adam's frequent calls. She'd carry the slips to her office, stare at them a few moments, then toss them in the wastebasket.

Each time she was tempted to call him back, she would think about the lessons she'd learned in the past, grit her teeth and get back to work. Though he wasn't far from her thoughts all week, she felt relieved to hear that he wasn't expected at the auction. Sylvie had done a little research and reported that he'd been invited but had sent his regrets, along with a generous donation for the children's charity.

Meredith left work early on Friday so that she had enough time to get ready for her big night onstage. As she entered her apartment and gave Lucy a hello pat, she felt as if a brick had lodged in her stomach. How in the world would she ever manage to go through with this? She forced herself not to think about the evening ahead and got into the shower. With the same determined mind set, she managed to get herself dressed. She was grateful now that Sylvie had offered to do her hair and makeup. Her hands were shaking so badly she was sure she would never have managed it.

Meredith stepped into the black satin heels, then sat down on her bed, staring blankly into space. She suddenly knew the true meaning of cold feet. Her entire body felt frozen with fear.

There was no help for it. She couldn't do it.

She would pack a small bag, stick Lucy in the back seat of her car and leave town for the weekend. Sylvie would be disappointed. She'd be livid, in fact. But after the smoke cleared, she'd understand.

Wouldn't she?

A sharp knock sounded on Meredith's door, jarring her from her escape plans. "Coming," Meredith called out. She fully expected it to be Sylvie at the door, stopping by to check up. But she was pleased and relieved to see that it was Rose Carson.

Although she hadn't seen Rose all week, Rose had heard from Sylvie that Meredith had been working overtime on an important assignment. Rose knew that when Meredith was tired, she wouldn't bother to eat, so she'd thoughtfully left some of her delicious home cooking at Meredith's front door. One night Meredith had found a dish of delectable fried chicken, homemade coleslaw and biscuits, and the next night, a pan of lasagna that was enough for three dinners. Meredith often thought of Rose as the mother she'd never had. Or, perhaps, the one she'd always wished for. While the two women had grown close over the years, Rose was also very respectful of Meredith's need for emotional distance. Her affection and concern made Meredith feel cared for but never smothered.

Meredith greeted Rose with a quick hug and welcomed her inside. "I was going to call, then I thought I'd just come up," Rose said. "Oh, my goodness, you look absolutely beautiful," Rose exclaimed, surveying Meredith from head to toe.

"So do you," Meredith replied sincerely.

Meredith had never seen her friend in such formal dress before and was surprised at the transformation. While Rose always looked attractive, tonight she looked positively aristocratic. Dressed in an elegant silver gown with a draped neckline trimmed in silver satin, her hair and makeup were much more elaborate than usual, but not at all overdone.

She was still a very lovely woman, Meredith noticed, not for the first time. She wondered why Rose had never remarried. But she had never asked her.

"Thank you, dear. I like to dress up once in a while. It's fun, don't you think?"

"Maybe...if all I had to look forward to was sipping champagne all night. But getting up on stage and participating in this auction thing..." Meredith sighed and pushed back a lock of hair that fell to her shoulders in a damp curly tumble. "I can't do it, Rose. I really can't."

Rose looked at her for a long moment, saying nothing. Then she took Meredith's hand in both of her own. "I know you're feeling some stage fright, Meredith. That's to be expected." Rose met her glance. "I know the auction idea is basically silly. I certainly agree with you there. But it is for a good cause, and, you know, I think this will be an experience for you, dear. Don't think about it as a serious thing. Do it just for fun."

"I'd rather have a root canal, just for fun," Meredith glanced at her and couldn't help but grin.

"Come on, Merri," Rose replied, using the nickname only Rose was allowed to use. "Don't think about Sylvie. Or even the charity. Do it for yourself. It's a chance for you to spread your wings a little. To show off a bit. Think of yourself as an actress, playing a part. Didn't you ever wish to be somebody else—a daring, reckless flirt? Breaking hearts left and right?'' Rose teased her. ''Well, tonight is your chance.''

''Yes, that's me. The big heartbreaker,'' Meredith murmured. Still, she could feel Rose's subtle persuasion melting down her resistance.

''Come on, now. You've got eyes in your head. You must know how gorgeous you are,'' Rose insisted. ''I'm sure you'll be the hit of the evening. And who knows, you just might meet the man of your dreams.''

''Someone better warn him I turn back into a pumpkin at the stroke of midnight,'' Meredith replied lightly.

Besides, she'd already met him, she wanted to say. But she'd sent him away. Far away…

''Some men like apple pie…and some prefer pumpkin. That's what makes the world go around,'' Rose replied with a shrug. ''So, does that mean you'll do it?''

''You've got me, Rose,'' Meredith replied. She picked up her velvet wrap and slipped it around her shoulders. ''Besides, Sylvie will murder both of us if I don't show up, and I'd hate to see anything happen to you.''

''Don't worry about me, dear. I can take care of myself,'' Rose assured her with a twinkle in her eye. Sometimes Meredith had the oddest feeling that there was more to her older friend than there appeared to be. She couldn't say what mystery she suspected. But Rose had secrets, that much she felt for sure. But, then, don't we all, Meredith reminded herself.

''Oh, I almost forgot. The brooch you loaned me,'' Meredith said. She picked up the velvet box from the side table and opened it. ''I wanted to wear it tonight. Would you help me put it on?''

''With pleasure,'' Rose replied. She helped Meredith pin the brooch to the center of her low, heart-shaped neckline.

"The perfect touch," Rose pronounced, stepping back to admire her.

Meredith examined her reflection in the hallway mirror. The glittering piece looked as if it was made specifically for this dress.

Studying the brooch, Meredith felt almost hypnotized as her eye followed the flashes of color and light set off in the cluster of gems. It was almost as if some enchanted fairy-tale figure had dipped a hand into a pile of precious gems and offered them up as a magical talisman.

As Meredith gazed at the pin, she experienced a strange, uncanny feeling. As if cold fingers danced up her spine, causing her skin to break out in gooseflesh.

Just nerves about tonight, she told herself. But still…

"The dress…it's not…too low, do you think?" she asked.

"Not at all," Rose assured her.

"The brooch is beautiful. Thank you again for letting me borrow it." Meredith leaned over and gave Rose a quick kiss on the cheek. "Where did you get it? Was it a gift?"

"Oh, that's a long story, dear. I'll tell you someday. Although I will tell you that it's always brought me luck…. Look," Rose held up her watch for Meredith to see the time. "It's getting late. I promised Sylvie I'd have you there by half past seven. We'd better go."

"Yes, I guess we'd better," Meredith agreed. She opened her small silk clutch, checked the contents, then snapped it closed. She was grateful that Rose had come. The older woman's quiet words had calmed Meredith's nerves, and the pin had somehow given her courage. As if she now carried Rose's good wishes and warm spirit with her.

As they rode down in the elevator together, Meredith once again found herself touching the pin lightly with her fingertips, as if it were a secret talisman. She glanced at Rose and saw her small, knowing smile. Maybe she'd make it through the evening after all, Meredith thought....

When Meredith and Rose arrived at the hotel, they found the lobby crowded with people attending the auction. They located the ballroom, then Meredith left Rose to look for Sylvie backstage, as she had been instructed.

After Sylvie did her hair and makeup in a dressing room backstage, Meredith was free to wander around the cocktail hour. Just as all her friends had predicted, she suddenly found herself a virtual man-magnet. The attention from the opposite sex was nearly overwhelming. Men were actually gazing at her with strange, dazed expressions on their faces. Sometimes their mouths would even drop open. Several men she'd never met before boldly attempted to start up a conversation, but she quickly slipped away from all of them. There was also a co-worker, a salesman named Rob Reilly who prided himself on his reputation as a superstud and came on with all the subtlety of a bulldozer. Meredith found that conversation particularly amusing, since Rob had never shown her the slightest interest before. After a few moments it became apparent that Mr. Studly hadn't recognized her from the office, and Meredith enjoyed playing him along and then announcing her identity. His sheer shock was partly amusing...and partly hurtful. Was she actually that bad in real life? she wondered.

But she quickly shrugged off the feeling and, as Rose had advised, she had fun with the role of femme fatale. While it had never been her fantasy to be a drop-dead gorgeous knockout, playing the role was truly amusing. Meredith was partly flattered, partly amused and partly...shocked by the male reaction. Were men so shallow that all it took was a layer of makeup and a push-up bra to turn the pack of them into drooling fools? Wasn't any man attracted by the size of a woman's brain...and not her breasts?

Meredith returned backstage, convinced that she wasn't going to meet her Prince Charming in this bunch of bachelors. Not if the cocktail hour had been any sample.

Meredith was second on the auction list, and she stood backstage near the curtain, feeling breathless and dizzy as she watched the bidding progress on the first young woman who took center stage. She'd carefully limited herself to only one glass of champagne, but since she hadn't eaten any lunch the drink had gone straight to her head. As she listed forward on her very high heels she felt the alcohol's effect. She pressed her hand to her forehead, feeling a bit dizzy.

"...and our next young lady is an employee of Colette, Inc. A jewelry designer named Meredith Blair," she heard the master of ceremonies say. That was her cue to step out onstage, she knew. But Meredith felt her feet frozen in place.

"Meredith, are you okay?" Meredith turned to see Sylvie staring at her with concern.

Meredith said nothing, but simply stared back. Sylvie took her arm and led her to the edge of the curtain. "Come on, Meredith, you can do it," Sylvie assured her.

"But, I—" Meredith had no time to finish her reply. With a friendly but firm push, Meredith found herself projected out from behind the curtain, stumbling backward.

The MC gracefully caught her arm and led her to the mark on the stage, right behind the microphone.

''Isn't she a beauty?'' he asked the audience. The answering reply, a chorus of male hoots, wolf whistles and catcalls made Meredith blush from head to toe.

''Look out at the audience, not at your shoes, dear,'' the MC whispered, carefully covering the microphone. ''You know, flaunt it a little,'' he instructed her.

Flaunt it? Meredith thought the man should feel fortunate she wasn't running for the nearest exit. She looked up into the bright lights and found she could barely make out any faces in the audience. An unexpected blessing, she decided as the bidding began. She took a deep breath and felt the makeshift fastener on her too tight décolletage threaten to pop. That would get the bidding going, she thought with a wry grin.

But the bids were already flying fast and furious. Meredith was amazed as the dollar figure climbed higher. All for a few hours of her charming company, she reminded herself with a secret grin. The dollar number grew very large, and it appeared that the matter was settled. Then suddenly a new bidder jumped in, offering a figure so large the audience grew silent and Meredith's mouth grew dry.

''Going once, going twice...'' the MC said. No other bidders challenged. Meredith's thoughts spun. The ordeal was almost over...or had it just begun? Who in the world was going to pay that astronomical sum for her?

''Sold!'' the MC shouted. ''Well done, sir. You have excellent taste, I might add. You may collect your prize backstage. And, have a wonderful evening,'' he added, causing the crowd to jeer.

With flushed cheeks, Meredith fled off the stage, managing not to tumble in her heels or knock over the many flower arrangements that decorated the stage.

Finally she stood backstage again, in the blessed darkness. She felt mostly numb, in shock from the ordeal. As she waited, someone thrust a bottle of champagne into her hands—an additional prize for her bidder—but Meredith barely noticed. Her heart pounding, she waited to face the man who would claim her. The deep, confident voice had sounded vaguely familiar, though she couldn't quite match the voice with a face. Was it someone she worked with? she wondered as she peered into the backstage shadows.

Then all of a sudden she felt a hand on her bare shoulder. "Meredith?"

She spun and found herself staring up at Adam Richards. Dressed in a black tuxedo with a brilliant white shirt and burgundy tie, he looked every inch the millionaire out on the town.

Didn't Sylvie promise her that he wasn't going to attend? Well, no help for it now. At least the man who had bought her was due to arrive any second. Out of the frying pan...into the fire.

"Adam..." she said. "What...what are you doing back here?"

He smiled and met her startled gaze. It was a slow, knowing smile that gave her goose bumps.

"I was told to come backstage and claim my prize. Don't you remember?" he replied simply. He was still staring at her, drawing closer but not smiling now at all.

Meredith felt as if she couldn't breathe.

No, it couldn't be.

There had to be some mistake. Adam Richards had *not* been her highest bidder.

But the look on his darkly handsome face confirmed her deepest fear.

"No, not you...." Meredith sighed and pressed her hand to her forehead. "Anyone but you," she blurted out.

"Meredith, you're so honest," he laughed. "My poor ego will just have to get used to it, I guess."

Meredith suddenly realized how she'd sounded. "Oh, I'm sorry. I didn't mean to insult you." She met his warm, dark gaze, and her voice faltered. Onstage she heard another young woman being auctioned off. The audience started clapping and stomping. The sound was deafening. Meredith felt as if she couldn't stand another minute of it.

"Come on. Let's get out of here." Adam leaned toward her and whispered in her ear. "You look like you could use a little fresh air."

He put his arm around her waist, and she allowed him to hold her close as he led her through the bustling backstage crowd. It felt good walking beside him, not even bothering to think as his tall commanding figure cut a path for them, his hold sheltering her.

Finally they were in the hotel corridor just outside the big ballroom. Meredith paused and took a breath. She glanced up at him. "Thank you," she said shyly. "I guess I'm just not cut out for show business."

He smiled and stepped back, his arm slipping off her shoulder. He's a gentleman, she thought, not pressing his advantage. His arm around her shoulders had felt awfully good, though, she had to admit.

"I don't know about that. I think you did very well up there. And you do look the role entirely. Absolutely stunning, I must say," he added in a serious tone. His gaze took her in from head to toe. Meredith was admittedly naive, but the look of arousal in his eyes was unmistakable.

For some reason his compliment—and reaction—got under her skin. Instead of feeling pleased, she was annoyed. Here she was, all this time, thinking he might be different from the rest. But a dash of red lipstick and a little cleavage had him showing his true colors after all, she thought.

"I'll bet you didn't recognize me," she replied tartly, adjusting her wrap so that it covered her bare shoulders and neckline.

"You almost had me fooled," he admitted. "But I suppose I recognized you in the nick of time, didn't I?"

Meredith carefully avoided meeting his gaze. "Well, I hope you're not disappointed, but it's just a fancy dress. A borrowed dress I might add. And some makeup. It's the same old me underneath," she warned him.

"I truly hope so," he said quietly. He leaned back against the wall and crossed his arms over his chest, watching her in a way that made her nervous.

Meredith finally looked up at him. "Why did you bid on me?" she asked point-blank.

She could barely believe she'd been so bold, and felt good about her courage. Maybe Rose was right. Maybe playing the glamour queen had boosted her confidence.

His brow creased as he considered her question. "That's a good question," he replied. Then he didn't answer for a long time. "I guess so that nobody else would," he admitted. "You looked distinctly uncomfortable up there. Bravely doing your part for a worthy cause, and all that. But..."

"So you decided to rescue me, you mean?"

"I didn't think of it that way," he replied, "but you could say that, I guess."

Had she really looked so awkward, so lacking in poise that Adam had been compelled to rescue her? Meredith was actually grateful, but now felt embarrassed.

"I really don't approve of these human auction things," he said, and Meredith felt he was being truthful, not just saying it because he thought it was what she wanted to hear. "I know it's for a worthy cause, but I hadn't even planned to attend."

That much she knew was true, as well.

"But you did," she said.

"Yes, I did. And the rest is history." He smiled broadly.

She took a deep breath. If she kept on staring into his eyes like this, she'd be lost. Get a grip, Meredith, she coached herself.

"So...what happens next?" she asked.

"Why don't you tell me? Would you like to go out to dinner, or have a drink someplace?"

Both alternatives were equally terrifying to Meredith. She didn't know what to say, and yet, she didn't want to seem completely thrown by his casual invitations. He was entitled to some socializing with her. Especially after the sum he'd paid. But she wouldn't be the one to decide.

"It's your evening," she replied. "I'm just the take-home prize," she quipped.

She hadn't meant the comment as a come-on, but once she said the words aloud—and watched Adam's thoughtful expression grow serious—she quickly realized how provocative she sounded.

"I guess I'll just take you home, then," he said, offering his arm. "My car's parked out front. We need to go down to the main lobby."

Meredith swallowed hard and wound her arm through

his. Did he mean back to his house, or back to hers? He really didn't seem like the predatory type...and yet, did he believe he bought and paid for something more than an hour or two of friendly...conversation?

"Meredith, your hands are like ice," he remarked, folding her fingers in his large palm. "Would you like my jacket?"

"No, I'm fine. Really," she assured him. They were standing in the large, ornate lobby, and Adam handed his parking voucher to a bellman.

When the car arrived, Adam escorted her out and helped her into the passenger side of the sleek black sports car. Meredith had never ridden in a car like this before. This was a night for firsts, she thought. Low to the ground, there was only room for the driver and one passenger. The leather bucket seats were comfortable, and she was surprised that her long legs fit comfortably as well. She dropped the bottle of champagne to the floor near her feet and made herself comfortable. The instrument panel looked like the dashboard of the space shuttle, she noticed, and she wondered if Adam could really tell what all the dials indicated.

Adam started the engine and steered the car down the crowded hotel driveway. Meredith sat back in her seat and tried to feign an air of composure...though she still had no idea of where they were going.

Four

"So, where to?" he asked.

"Excuse me?" she said.

"How do we get to your house from here? Do you live in town?" he asked as he deftly steered the car into the heavy midtown traffic.

"Uh...yes. Yes, I do. It's not far from here at all," she assured him. She breathed a silent prayer of gratitude. So he didn't think he was taking her back to his house. That was some relief. "I live on Amber Court, near Ingalls Park. Do you know how to get there?"

"That's a great neighborhood. I love it up there," he said. "I love the park. I go for long walks there or jog on the path around the lake."

"So do I," Meredith said. "I usually take Lucy. She doesn't keep pace with me that well, but she loves it."

"Lucy? Is that a friend of yours?"

Meredith was about to explain that Lucy was her dog,

then realized this could work to her advantage. ‘‘Uh… yes. A friend. A very good friend,’’ she stammered. ‘‘We live together.’’

‘‘Oh, so you have a roommate.’’

Was she imagining it, or was Adam disappointed to learn that she didn’t live alone? Meredith suppressed a small smile.

‘‘Yes, we share the apartment.’’ It wasn’t entirely a lie, she consoled herself. Terribly misleading…but not really a lie. ‘‘She’s a real pal. I’m sure she’s waiting up for me.’’

Lucy was most likely deeply asleep and maybe even snoring, Meredith guessed. But she did so want to give Adam the wrong idea.

‘‘It’s important to have good friends. It’s good to share your experiences with someone at the end of the day, don’t you think?’’ he asked.

‘‘Yes, of course. It is a good thing,’’ she replied quietly. She was not thinking of Lucy now, but of him. Imagining coming home to him and sharing her day. How silly, she thought, brushing the errant fantasy out of her mind. She stared out the window and watched the midtown street pass in a blur. Then she turned back to look at him.

In the small car their faces were very close. He was so utterly handsome. So strong and masculine. When she was near to him like this, she felt herself succumbing to the intense pull of his energy, his attraction, like a powerful tide pulling her under the sea. He didn’t have to do anything special. He didn’t have to say anything. Somehow, it was just…him. That was the mystery of it for her. The mystery—and the bare truth that scared her right down to her very soul.

They were driving alongside the park and came to the

turn for Amber Court. ‘‘Here’s the turn,’’ she announced. ‘‘Just make a right. My building is the middle of the street, number twenty.’’

He parked the car and helped her out. Meredith withdrew her keys and opened the heavy outside door that led to the lobby. ‘‘Well, you probably need to get going, so good-night,’’ she said, turning toward him. He was standing very close. Close enough to lean over and kiss her…if he wanted to.

She took a step back and stared up at him. Then she realized she was still carrying the bottle of champagne. ‘‘Oh, here. I almost forgot,’’ she said, handing it to him. ‘‘Part of your prize.’’

‘‘Thanks.’’ He took the bottle without looking at it, his gaze fixed on hers. ‘‘And, no, I have no place to be. I’d really like to continue our date. But I don’t care for champagne…would you like to take it?’’

She shook her head. ‘‘I don’t like it much, either. It usually gives me a headache.’’

He laughed. ‘‘Me, too.’’ Their eyes met and she suddenly felt weak at the knees.

‘‘How about coffee?’’ she asked quietly.

‘‘Coffee? That never gives me headache,’’ he replied.

‘‘No…I mean, would you like some?’’ she asked shyly.

He looked surprised. Then extremely pleased. His expression gave her a warm rush inside. ‘‘I’d love some coffee…if it’s not too much trouble for you?’’

‘‘No trouble at all,’’ she assured him as she led him through the lobby to the elevator.

‘‘Your roommate won’t mind?’’ he asked, glancing at his watch. ‘‘It is rather late.’’

‘‘Lucy won’t mind. She loves meeting new people.’’

‘‘I’d love to, then,’’ Adam replied. They stood in the

elevator side by side as it carried them up to the third floor. It was nearly midnight, Meredith noticed. The hour of enchantment in all the fairy tales.

She opened the door to her apartment and heard the gentle sound of the tags on Lucy's collar as the dog trotted out from the bedroom to greet them. "Hi, honey," Meredith said, crouching down to give Lucy a pat. "Did you sneak up on my bed again, sleepyhead?"

Lucy greeted Meredith with a quick lick but was clearly more interested in Adam. She sniffed his legs and hands, then licked him as he greeted her. "Hello, there. Aren't you a pretty dog," Adam said. He looked up at Meredith. "What's her name?"

Meredith stood up and straightened her gown. "Lucy," she said simply. She bit down on her lower lip as she watched his expression. He looked puzzled at first, then frowned. Then finally laughed. "Hello, Lucy," he said with even more enthusiasm. "I'm so happy to meet you, old girl."

Meredith laughed out loud as she walked into the kitchen and started filling the coffeepot. He had a good sense of humor, you had to grant him that, she thought.

"You have a great place," Adam said, appearing in the doorway. "I like the way you've decorated."

Meredith had never thought of herself as the homey type. The decor was rather minimal, with sleek modern furnishings, and a leather couch and chair. A patterned kilim area rug covered the polished hardwood floor. Posters from art exhibits along with a few of her own sculptures completed the rest of the decor. There was a space off the L-shaped living room for a dining area, but Meredith used it as a studio. She had another drawing table set up there and her supplies. Sometimes she brought work home from her job or worked on her own sculptures there, making sketches and models. Most of the actual pieces were quite large, however, and because they were made of welded metal, she rented a studio space in a warehouse downtown where she stored her materials and could use a blowtorch without worry.

As she carried a tray with the coffee things into the living room, she noticed that Adam was now looking around her studio. He returned to the living room and took a seat on the couch next to her. "Did you make the sculptures, Meredith?" he asked as he took a cup of coffee.

She nodded. "Most of them are a few years old. I'm working on much larger pieces now. In metal, mostly. I have some studio space in a warehouse near the river," she explained. "I go down there on the weekends or whenever I'm able."

"These designs are very interesting." He picked up one of the sculptures and examined it closer. "I like the sense of depth and the way the lines appear to flow upward," he said. "Do you sell your work through a gallery?"

Meredith smiled and shook her head. "I'm not that good. Honestly."

"Nonsense. You're very good. Very talented," he insisted. "I'd like to see more of your work. May I?"

She shrugged. "Of course. Maybe you could come down to my studio sometime," she added.

Sometime would never come, she was sure. Besides, he was just trying to be nice, to make friendly conversation.

Some makeup had gotten into her eye and Meredith dabbed it with a tissue.

"Something wrong?" Adam asked kindly. He leaned toward her, looking concerned.

"No, not at all," she replied still dabbing at her eye. "I'm just not used to wearing all this eye makeup."

"Why don't you get rid of it," he suggested. "I'll wait."

"Are you sure you don't mind? It may take a while," she warned him.

"Not at all. Besides, I have to admit, I like you better without all that...stuff on your face."

"I guess I don't pull off the supermodel look very well, do I?" she asked, deciding he must have meant the comment unkindly.

He reached out and took her hand. "That's not what I meant at all," he said quietly. "I'm sure you had fun tonight turning heads—and you certainly looked gorgeous. But you don't need the makeup, Meredith, or the low-cut gown, to be attractive. Besides, I don't think that Barbie-doll style is really you at all, is it?"

She peered up at him from lowered lashes, feeling secretly thrilled. "No...no it's not," she admitted with a small laugh.

"I don't find it very attractive," he added. "I like a little more mystery when I look at a woman. The way most of the women onstage tonight were dressed was a little too...obvious for me."

"Well, you must have been the only man there who felt that way," she replied.

"So be it," he said with a shrug. "I might be old-fashioned, but if I'm with a woman, I don't enjoy watching her baring all for the world to see. Some things should be saved for private moments, when two people are alone. Otherwise, an intimate relationship isn't that exclusive, is it?"

She didn't know what to say. Intimacy? Exclusivity? Relationships? How did they get onto this subject, for goodness sake? The very mention of such words made her practically jump off the couch.

"I'll be right back," she promised.

"No rush. I'll just sit here and have a nice talk with Lucy."

She laughed as she entered her bedroom and shut the door. She liked him. She liked him a lot. And he was here, in her house. Waiting for her in the next room. Just as she had imagined.

This was *not* a good scenario, Meredith decided as she pulled down her elaborate hairdo. She scrubbed off her makeup in record time and changed from her gown into a sweater and jeans. She considered putting on her glasses, then decided to leave the contacts in. She'd been practicing a few hours a day with them so she could wear them for the auction, and they still felt comfortable. If she could wear them instead of her glasses from time to time, that would be one benefit from tonight's comedy of errors, Meredith thought as she prepared to go back out to Adam.

She'd just make a little more chitchat with him, then convince him to go. He'd be nice about it and leave without a problem...wouldn't he?

When Meredith returned to the living room, Lucy was sitting next to Adam, her head resting on his knee and her eyes half-closed as he petted her.

"She really is a great dog," he said, looking up at Meredith.

"She's a peach," Meredith replied. "Though she usually doesn't take to strangers so quickly." Even dogs love him, she thought silently.

"More coffee, Adam?" she asked as she sat down again. If he didn't want more coffee, she'd soon start yawning and hinting for him to go.

"No more for me, thanks." He turned toward her, and she noticed that he'd unfastened his silk tie and the top buttons of his shirt. The tie hung loose around his neck, and she could see just a hint of the dark mat of hair on his chest. Her mouth went dry and she quickly turned away.

"I wonder what the other high bidders and their 'prizes' are doing now," he said, glancing at his watch.

"Yes, I wonder," Meredith agreed. She looked down at her lap. She had at first been horrified to find that Adam had won her...and now realized it had been a blessing in disguise. He didn't seem to have any expectations that his contribution had bought special favors. Not like some of the other men in the audience that she might have gotten stuck with, she guessed. She recalled the predatory looks she'd endured at the cocktail party and shuddered to imagine the possibilities.

"By the way...thank you for bidding on me. I've gotten off pretty easily, I guess."

"Don't mention it." He smiled at her, white teeth flashing against tanned skin. He leaned back and folded his arms behind his head, the muscles in his arms bunched under the thin fabric of his shirt. "I'll consider it this week's chivalrous act," he added. "Besides, the night's not over yet."

His seductive, teasing tone made her nerve endings tingle. No, it wasn't over until it was over, as they said at the ball park. Right?

She cleared her throat and sat up a bit straighter. Had he moved closer to her on the couch...or had she imagined that?

"I've done you a fairly nice favor tonight, I think," he said. "And now you can do me one, Meredith."

"I can? What exactly did you have in mind?" Her

voice sounded prim, even to her own ears. But Meredith couldn't help it.

He laughed. "Nothing indecent, I promise you. I want you to work on my account again. That's all," he said. "The sample stickpin you made was perfect."

"Thanks. I'm glad you liked it," she said sincerely. She felt pleased that he liked her work so much. "But I can't work on the other pieces, honestly, Adam. I'm in the middle of a big assignment. Samples for a new line. A complete collection. I was told to focus on it totally."

"Yes, that's what the other designer told me...what was her name again? Andrea?"

"*Anita,*" she corrected in a clipped tone. So, Anita had been assigned to Adam's work. Meredith felt a wave of jealousy rush over her and then felt annoyed by her reaction.

"Yes, that's what Anita told me. But why didn't you answer any of my calls?"

"I'm sorry...I was really very busy this week and I knew that someone else had been assigned to work with you."

He looked genuinely hurt that she had avoided speaking to him, and suddenly she wished she had called him back, if only to explain her situation.

"And the sweater set," he added, "You didn't need to return that to me. Didn't you like it?"

"Of course I did. It was beautiful. I loved it," she answered honestly.

"Then why did you send it back to me?" he asked, sounding genuinely puzzled. He sat upright again and ran his hand through his thick, dark hair. His hair looked so soft and full, for an instant she was tempted to do the same.

Meredith turned away. It was hard to concentrate with him sitting so close. His every movement, his every breath distracted her.

"The gift was very extravagant and...totally unnecessary," she said, trying to frame her words very carefully.

"The best ones usually are, Meredith," he replied with a mild laugh.

She turned and met his gaze. "I felt it was inappropriate. Considering our relationship."

"Not businesslike and impersonal you mean?" His deep voice had taken on a more serious tone. But she still felt as if he was secretly teasing her.

"Yes, that's right," she said.

"Well, if you won't work on my account anymore, then we're not in a business relationship, Meredith. So you still could have kept the gift."

He grinned playfully at her, and Meredith simply stared back, then pressed her hand to her forehead. He was talking circles around her, and her head was spinning.

"I can't work on your account, Adam. As I said, I'm on a special project. A superrush job."

"I'll wait until that's over. If it's as superrush as you say, it should be done soon, right?"

He seemed to have an answer for everything when he wanted his way, she noticed. Well, that's how you got to be successful and rich, right? Not by giving up easily, she reflected.

"I'm very flattered. Honestly," she replied. "But the other designers in my department are both very, very good. I'm sure Anita will do exactly what you want."

Exactly what he wanted in and out of the office, Meredith had no doubt.

"I'm sure she's good at her work. But not as good as you. And you don't do exactly as I want, Meredith. You do what *you* want...and it turns out infinitely better than anything I could ever have suggested. That's the difference."

"Thank you."

She felt worn down by his arguments...and her own attraction to him. She didn't like the idea of not seeing him again. If she passed off his work, she knew in her heart she wouldn't have a moment's peace, thinking about him and Anita.

"I guess I can work on the other pieces for you. I'll just have to persuade my boss that I can manage both assignments," she said impulsively.

"Terrific. I was hoping I could convince you." His pleased expression told her that there was no turning back.

"Well, I do owe you a favor... For tonight, I mean."

"Yes, you do. Let's consider it all square now, all right?"

She nodded. He was still staring deeply into her eyes, and she felt her heartbeat race. His face was so close she could feel the heat of his body and inhale the subtle spicy scent of his skin.

Meredith didn't know what to say. He moved closer and slipped his arm around her shoulder. She meant to move away from him, but as he stared into her eyes, she was mesmerized. He reached out and gently moved a curl of her hair that had fallen across her eyes.

"I love the color of your hair," he said quietly, holding the lock between his fingers for a moment longer than was necessary. "It's so unusual. I'm not even going to ask if it's natural, because I'm sure it is," he added with a smile. "Everything about you is so real. So genuine...and beautiful."

Adam's simple words touched her deeply. First of all she knew he was being totally sincere. Not just saying what he thought she wanted to hear. But more than that, she felt as if he saw the real her, not the social mask she was forced to wear. He looked past the wrapping and saw the person she was deep inside...and he was truly attracted to that person. The thought was somehow astounding to her.

She reached up and touched his cheek, amazed at his slow, pleased smile. When he leaned toward her and their lips met, she wasn't at all surprised. She realized that she had been wanting him to kiss her for a very long time, maybe even from the first minute they had met.

The touch of his lips on hers was thrilling.

Intoxicating.

Overwhelming.

Before she could even consider pulling away, her senses were overwhelmed, and her compelling attraction erased her apprehensions.

His kiss was not the least bit tentative or questioning. He pressed his mouth to hers, savoring the taste and touch of her lips. As he felt her surrender to his touch, she heard his deep, hungry moan, and his arms moved around her in a tight embrace. He kissed her hungrily and her mouth opened under his, their tongues melding and merging in a swirling, passionate dance.

She felt as if she was melting into him, weightless and mindless as waves of pure feeling washed away her doubts and inhibitions. As Adam's kisses grew deeper, Meredith leaned back against the couch and soon found her body stretched out beneath his. His firm touch moved down her arms and breasts, caressing and stroking her body, her waist, hips and flat stomach.

She needed to touch him, too, to feel his firm muscles and warm skin beneath the fabric of his shirt and pants. He felt so good, so warm and real. His mouth moved from her lips, down the sensitive line of her throat to the bare skin exposed by the V-neckline of her sweater. He pulled the sweater aside, exposing her bare shoulder and chest. He softly kissed the top of her breasts, his fingertips slipping beneath her sweater to caress her breasts to throbbing fullness as he stroked her hardened nipples.

Meredith felt her body shudder as a hot wave of desire flooded through her limbs. Her hands, which had been moving across his back, now gripped him hard as she pressed her face into his shoulder and shifted her hips restlessly next to him. His mouth moved over hers again, kissing her deeply. She kissed him back, answering his longing. He shifted slightly, so that their lower bodies were pressed together, heat against heat. She felt the hard evidence of his longing for her pressed against her thigh, and she moved even closer, fitting their bodies together in a shadow dance of lovemaking.

What was he doing to her? some distant voice in her mind screamed.

What had begun as a simple good-night kiss had instantly escalated into a nuclear meltdown. Like a match held to a pile of tinder, it took just a single kiss to send her entirely up in flames.

This is the way it had started with Jake. One kiss, and she was his, body and soul. It had come over her so quickly, she'd never had time to stop and think, to consider the consequences. Not that it would have mattered. She'd trusted Jake implicitly…and she'd trusted her own feelings.

But she knew better now. Far better.

And though her desire for Adam was even stronger than her longing for Jake had ever been, some dim, rational part of Meredith's mind managed to summon up the willpower to pull away.

Adam immediately sensed her withdrawal. He lifted his head and looked at her. "Meredith? Are you okay?"

She was lying beneath him, her head turned to the side. She sighed and pressed her hands against his shoulders. "This isn't right.... This is not what I want. Let me get up. Please."

He looked surprised at her request, but immediately pulled away from her and sat up. He let out a long, slow breath and moved his hand through his hair.

"I'm sorry," he said finally. He glanced over at her. "I just wanted to kiss you good-night...I didn't mean for things to go so far. The last thing I wanted to do was scare you."

She sensed that he yearned to reach out and touch her again, a soothing, reassuring touch—but thought better of it.

Meredith stood up and took a few steps away from him. She didn't want him to see how deeply his kisses and closeness had affected her. He didn't need to know how much she wanted him, she reasoned. That would only make it harder for her.

"You didn't scare me," she said finally. It's my own response to you that scares me, she added silently.

"I like you, Adam. I really do. But I don't want to get involved with you in that way."

His dark brows rose in a look of surprise. "Really? That's not the way it seemed a few minutes ago."

"I can't quite explain that," she said, though in truth she simply didn't want to. "You'll just have to take me at my word. Or we can't have any type of relationship at all.''

A serious expression fell over his face. She wondered if he was angry with her. Considering the way she had responded to him, he had every right to be, she thought.

''Do you have a boyfriend or something? Are you involved with someone else?'' he asked.

''A boyfriend? No, I don't have a boyfriend,'' she said, shaking her head. ''That's not it at all,'' she assured him.

He didn't say anything at first, just continued to gaze at her. Then he rose and picked up his jacket. He looked a bit tired, she thought, with his tousled hair and five-o'clock shadow, but even more handsome and desirable, if that was possible.

''All right,'' he said slowly. ''I guess I'll be off then.''

All this time she'd been hoping he would leave. But now that he was actually going, she felt surprised and as if she really didn't want to see him go. Don't be ridiculous, she scolded herself.

He headed for the door and she followed. When he reached her front door and opened it, she noticed how he carefully avoided brushing against her.

''Good night, Meredith.'' He paused and shrugged his broad shoulders into his jacket. ''I'll be speaking to you.''

She searched his expression. He wasn't mad at her, as she had thought, she decided. He looked quite calm. Resigned was a more accurate word perhaps. Had he accepted her terms? Knowing how persistent he could be, she doubted it. More as if he knew he'd lost the battle…but would return to fight another day.

So be it, Meredith thought. They were not going to solve this tonight.

"By the way," he added as he stepped into the hallway, "I'm glad I decided to use that ticket tonight after all. It turned out to be a very interesting evening."

She knew it wasn't the time to be provocative, but she couldn't stop herself. "Did you get your money's worth after all then?"

"Without a doubt. This just may turn out to be the best investment I ever made." He flashed a sexy grin, and Meredith felt a warm blush rise up to color her cheeks.

Darn you, Adam Richards. She couldn't stand feeling so vulnerable around him. So vulnerable around any man.

He looked annoyingly smug, she thought, as he turned and strolled down the hallway. She quickly slammed shut her door.

Five

All weekend long Meredith wondered if she would hear from Adam again. She kept her answering machine on, just in case, so that she wouldn't have to speak to him. Yet, when he didn't call, she felt unaccountably disappointed. Maybe in the cold light of day, he had decided he didn't want to get involved with her after all. A man like Adam could have most any woman he wanted. He didn't need to get hung up on someone who was clearly a walking romantic obstacle course.

By Monday morning Meredith had convinced herself that she'd never hear from Adam again, not even in regard to his account at Colette. She was a bit surprised when Anita Barnes walked into her office to return Meredith's sketches and notes on Adam's work. It seemed that Adam had called Frank directly and arranged everything. Anita looked a bit miffed as she made her delivery, but Meredith ignored her. Better luck next time, she murmured under her breath as the other designer swiveled out of her office.

So, he hadn't been totally turned off after all, Meredith realized. But had he taken her at her word and accepted that she didn't want to get emotionally involved with him? Only time would tell.

While Adam was very respectful of her deadline on the Everlasting Collection, Meredith knew that she could work on both projects at once, and she called his office Monday afternoon to set up their next meeting.

She felt nervous to call him, with thoughts of the torrid kisses they'd shared on Friday night racing through her mind as she dialed his number. She had hoped that his secretary would arrange the appointment, but as soon as Meredith announced her name, she was immediately put on hold. The next thing she knew, Adam was on the line.

"Adam? It's me, Meredith. I've been reassigned to your project."

"How nice to hear your voice. I was just thinking of you," Adam greeted her.

Meredith struggled to keep a businesslike frame of mind. Did he have to say things like that to her all the time? It totally threw her off.

"Yes, well…I'm just calling to set up an appointment. What day is good for you?"

"Hmm, let's see…." She heard him shuffling some papers around and assumed he was looking for his calendar. "This week looks very busy. I'll be out of town starting tomorrow until Friday…."

Meredith remained silent. Maybe she'd get out of seeing him again this week. That would be a relief. By the time they met again, she might have more control of her attraction to him.

"How about tonight? I could come by your office, say around six o'clock. We could have dinner."

"Tonight? I usually don't have meetings like this after working hours," she replied.

"Perhaps you could make an exception," he gently suggested. "Otherwise, I'm afraid I won't be able to get together with you until the weekend."

"The weekend? Oh, no. I couldn't do it over the weekend." She knew she sounded horrified by the prospect, but she couldn't help it.

"Oh, do you have plans?"

She did have plans. But not socializing, if that's what he meant. She'd planned to work in her studio at the warehouse so she could finish a large sculpture she'd started some weeks ago. There was a juried show coming up, and she'd hoped to enter it.

"I really can't do it on the weekend, so I guess we'll have to meet tonight."

Adam sounded pleased to have gotten his way... again, she noticed. They agreed to meet at her office at six, and Meredith considered running out at lunchtime to buy a new outfit. She was wearing a forest-green cotton knit dress that had long sleeves and rounded neckline. The familiar dress had seemed a comfortable choice this morning...but now seemed awfully drab. Then she squelched the idea of primping for him. He claimed to like her just the way she was, with no extra effort necessary. Well, here she was, in all her genuine glory.

She had experimented today, wearing her contact lenses to work. Meredith felt very self-conscious about not wearing her glasses, but the change in her appearance was probably quite subtle, she realized. Some people had noticed something different about her today but couldn't quite figure out what it was. The receptionist thought perhaps she'd gotten a new hairdo. It made Meredith realize that it was foolish to feel self-conscious. Most people actually didn't notice much about others, they were too busy thinking about themselves.

Adam, however, seemed to notice everything about her. Down to the tiniest freckle. It was unnerving and flattering at the same time.

After this meeting she wouldn't have to have much contact with him in order to complete his work. She could get through a few more hours with him—without giving in to her attraction for him—couldn't she? She'd just have to make sure they met in a restaurant...and didn't return to her place for coffee again.

Just a few minutes before five-thirty, Meredith put her work aside and got ready to meet Adam. That morning she had quickly brushed her hair back and secured it in a large clip, but now she decided to wear it in a long braid instead. Not a huge difference, but a bit more becoming, she thought. She added some lip gloss and a dash of eye shadow and mascara, a gift from Sylvie for helping out at the auction. Just as she was closing her purse, she found the velvet box that contained Rose's brooch. She had planned to stop by Rose's apartment tonight to return it in person. The jeweled pin was certainly far too precious to leave outside Rose's door or even in her mailbox.

Meredith flipped open the lid and studied the pin again. The design was really quite unique, and she would guess it was one of a kind and not a mass-manufactured item. From her experience, she also guessed it was perhaps a sample piece or prototype, probably crafted by some designer like herself. She wondered about the person who had made it. How had Rose come across it, she wondered? Maybe as a gift? Rose had said it was a long story, and Meredith resolved to ask her about it.

On impulse Meredith removed the pin and fastened it to her dress. The rich-green fabric was the perfect backdrop for the brooch and complimented the simple style of her dress.

Meredith was clearing off her drawing table and packing some work to take home when she heard a sharp knock just outside her office door and turned to see Adam in the doorway. He had on a dark blue suit, white shirt and patterned silk tie and looked very corporate, she thought. And very handsome.

"I didn't mean to startle you." He smiled at her and walked into the office. "The receptionist was gone, so I just came back and started looking for you."

"Well, here I am," she said lightly. He was still smiling down at her, that gentle, warm smile of his that made her feel as if she had suddenly stepped out into the sun. She pulled her gaze away from his and picked up her large, square leather tote, which was better than a briefcase for carrying her sketchpads and notebooks.

"Can I take that for you?" he offered politely.

"No thanks." She shook her head and clung to the bag as they left the office. She really needed something to hold on to right now. Something to put some distance between them.

They left the building and walked to a nearby restaurant Adam suggested. He thought it would be quiet and a good place to talk. Meredith had never eaten there, so she didn't know if it would be quiet. She'd heard of the place, though...and she knew it would be expensive.

The maître d' and waiters greeted Adam by name, and they were quickly given a secluded table with a view of the garden behind the restaurant. It was not exactly a business meeting atmosphere, Meredith thought as she strained to read the menu in the dim light. She had no doubt that Adam had purposely chosen this place to get her into a more romantic frame of mind. Everyone seemed to know him here. It was probably his favorite spot for romancing his dates. Of which he had many, she was sure.

But she couldn't give in to his tactics—or to her own desire for him. She'd already told him in no uncertain terms that she wouldn't get romantically involved with him. And she was determined to stick by that statement.

A waiter brought their drinks and they ordered dinner. As Adam sipped a glass of Merlot, Meredith pulled out her sketchpad and notebook, along with the file she'd made for his work, and placed them on the table next to her plate.

"So, what did you have in mind for the other pieces?" she asked, flipping open her pad.

Adam's full mouth twisted in a grin. For a moment she thought he might laugh out loud at her efforts to keep things businesslike.

"Where are those big, horn-rimmed glasses of yours, Meredith? Did you lose them somewhere?" he teased.

"I'm wearing contact lenses," she said. She looked down at her pad and fiddled with the pencil. "As if you didn't know that."

He laughed. "I'm just teasing you. I'm sorry." He reached across the table and took her hand. The contact was subtly electrifying and Meredith's gaze flew up and met his. "It's hard to resist. I love to make you blush."

She looked down and sighed. "I wish I didn't blush so easily," she confessed. "It's annoying."

"No it's not," he said. "It's wonderful. You have the most beautiful skin."

''And you definitely know how to get under it,'' Meredith admitted impulsively.

''Do I really?'' He laughed out loud, dimples deepening in his lean cheeks. ''Thank you, Meredith. I think that's the nicest thing you've ever said to me.''

She glanced at him. His sparkling dark eyes and warm expression were too much for her to take in for very long. She could just about feel her circuits overloading, the energy between them was so strong. She quickly glanced down at her glass of white wine. He still held her hand and now softly rubbed his fingers against hers. She felt her resolve quickly melting away. Like a pat of butter dropped on a hot pan.

''We'll get our work done, don't worry,'' he promised her.

''We'd better, or I'll be in trouble,'' she told him.

''Frank won't bother you. We're old friends.''

She wasn't sure she liked the idea of Adam running interference for her at work. But she was more curious about his relationship with Frank Reynolds.

''How do you know Frank?'' she asked.

''A few years ago I took some design courses at Taylor School of Art. Frank was one of my teachers. We got to be good friends.''

''You studied art?'' she asked, surprised at the news. While he certainly had good taste and an eye for color and form, she'd never taken him for the artistic type. To the contrary, she'd assumed he was all business, all the way.

''Just a few night courses. Back when I was starting my business. I needed to understand what designers were saying to me. You know sometimes you artistic types speak your own language.''

"Hmm, sometimes you business types do, too," she replied, meeting his warm gaze.

"Yes, I know. But when words fail we must resort to nonverbal communication," he said softly. He leaned over and kissed her gently on the lips, his hand coming up to cup her cheek. Meredith closed her eyes and savored the touch of his mouth on hers. She'd been secretly hungry for a kiss, for that special, tender contact. He began to pull away, his mouth lingering in a tantalizing way on hers. She could tell he wanted more. They both did.

He sat back and studied her reaction. "I'm sorry... you probably didn't want me to do that, did you?"

She raised her gaze to meet his and squeezed his hand. "Actually...I did," she admitted. "So you really don't need to apologize."

He smiled at her. "You're blushing again."

She sighed, and they both laughed. "Yes...I know."

As Meredith looked at Adam's strong profile, she felt suddenly guilty that in all the time they'd spent together so far, she'd never really asked him about his business or his background. He must have thought she was terribly self-centered. But that wasn't it at all.

All this time she'd been struggling to keep him at arm's length. But actually, she yearned to know everything about him. Every last, tiny detail. Where he grew up. If he preferred the city or the country. Lakes, or the seashore. When was his birthday? What was his middle name? His favorite dessert.

She wanted to know everything...but didn't dare say a word. It simply seemed too perfect between them, just then, to spoil it by talking. They sat in silence holding hands, and Meredith knew that she simply felt absolutely…content. And yet, at the same time, completely electrified. A feeling of true connection. And astonishing attraction. Adam was so good. So dear. He'd been so patient with her. That a man like Adam could be attracted to her was almost unbelievable to her. He was really impossible to resist.

And she was tired of trying.

The waiter soon arrived with the first course, and as they ate, Meredith had a chance to ask Adam about himself. As she had guessed, he grew up in the Midwest, in Greenbrier, Wisconsin, which he described as a dairy farming town. He had been the only boy in the family, with three younger sisters, which she suspected accounted for his protective attitude toward women. He certainly seemed to have a protective attitude toward her. His father had owned the local hardware store and he described his mother as devoted to her children…and now, her grandchildren. Meredith could tell by the way he spoke of his family that he had been raised in a loving, close home. She envied that.

Her home life as a child had been so vastly different. When he asked her about it, she had to admit that her strongest memories of childhood had been her parents fighting bitterly. Her mother had always resented giving up her acting career to marry and have a baby. Her father's demanding career in corporate law left him little time with his family. They were both very dramatic, emotional people, Meredith explained. They both had affairs and indiscretions, just to hurt each other, Meredith had always suspected. Their marriage was an emotional tug of war, and with their only child always stuck in the middle.

Her parents finally divorced when she was in college, and both seemed far happier now, she reported. Her father had retired and traveled a great deal with his second wife. Her mother had moved out to California and picked up her acting career. Meredith had never been sure why they stayed together unhappily for so long, though they always claimed it was for her sake.

"It must have been very hard for you," Adam said sympathetically.

"I survived. Some people have had it far worse growing up," she insisted. "I sometimes think that if I had grown up in a happy environment, I would have missed out on reading a lot of great books and never become so interested in art."

Adam begrudgingly agreed, but still regarded her with concern.

"All I wanted to do growing up was play baseball. I was outside from dawn to dusk, playing ball with my friends. Sometimes my father had to come and find me to bring me home, after dark."

"I guess almost every boy wants to be a professional baseball player at some point, right?"

"Darn right. It's carried in the Y chromosome, I'm sure of it," he joked.

Adam must have been a far better baseball player than most boys, Meredith realized. He'd attended the University of Wisconsin on a full athletic scholarship, where he earned a master's degree in business. He still had the lean, muscular build of an athlete, and she suspected he worked out to keep in shape.

She was curious to know how he started his business. He clearly didn't have the advantage of family money, and she wondered how he had managed to get so far so fast. Adam explained how he had decided to start his own company after working for a firm he thought was terribly disorganized and had not kept up with market trends. He saw thousands of young singles and new families in need of low-cost, stylish furniture and had ideas for catering to that market. But his employer, a rigid, family-owned company, wouldn't listen to him. So he decided to go off on his own. It was risky at first, and he encountered some setbacks raising enough capital. But he finally got the financing he needed and devoted himself to making the enterprise work.

"I was at the office night and day for the first few years," he confessed. "I even kept several changes of clothes on hand there. We were really short-staffed and sometimes after working all day at my desk, I'd have to drive a truck and make deliveries at night."

"You're kidding, right?" Meredith asked in disbelief.

"I wish I was…see these gray hairs?" he asked, pointing out the strands of silver at his brow. "Premature."

Meredith laughed. "Very distinguished I thought," she complimented him.

He smiled, then looked serious. "Kidding aside, it was hard to get things off the ground. More than a few times it looked pretty grim, and I thought I wouldn't make it. I know the long hours I spent in the office took a toll on my marriage."

"Oh…you were married?" Meredith was taken by surprise for a moment. Had he mentioned he'd been married? She was sure she would have remembered that.

"I married my college girlfriend. My only girlfriend, actually," he admitted with a small smile. "She wasn't very interested in the business, and I think she felt neglected."

"Was that why you divorced?" Meredith asked.

"Well, not entirely…there were a lot of reasons why it didn't work out." He paused and she could tell that he didn't want to discuss the details any further. "I envy people who have met in their twenties and manage to stay married fifty years or more. My folks are like that. They're still in love. You can just see it. I'd always hoped for that kind of marriage myself...but it didn't work out like that for us. Suzanne and I didn't grow together—we grew apart. In the end I hardly recognized her, our values and outlook were so radically different. Anyway, she lives in Europe now, and I think we're both happy with the way our lives turned out."

It was a sad story, Meredith thought. And a sobering one. His dark eyes were filled with regret as he tried to explain his failed marriage. It was unsettling to remember how a romance could start off seeming so permanent and indestructible...and end so painfully.

It was hard to try again after a disappointment like that. Meredith knew only too well. She hadn't suspected that Adam was battling his own ghosts of lovers past. Didn't that make their chances of success even slimmer?

"How about you, Meredith? Have you ever been married?" he asked.

The question took her by surprise. She looked up and met his serious gaze, then quickly looked away. "Married? Uh, no...not me," she said, shaking her head.

He leaned back and regarded her quietly for a moment. She hoped he was going to let the subject drop. But he didn't let her off the hook quite so easily.

"You're blushing again," he observed quietly, "so there must have been someone important in your life... Maybe, still in your life?"

"I'm not seeing anyone right now, if that's what you mean," she replied evenly. She folded her napkin and set it aside.

"But there was someone serious...and it didn't work out?"

"Something like that," she replied. "It was a long time ago. And I was very young and...naive."

"And he was older?" Adam guessed.

Her gaze flew up to meet his. "You're good at filling in the blanks."

"Maybe. But I'd much rather you tell me the story." The way he looked at her just then made her feel she could tell him anything—anything at all—and he wouldn't think any less of her or care any less about her.

That was a good feeling, Meredith realized. And an uncommon one, for her. Such unconditional approval and acceptance had been so rare in her life. Just about nonexistent.

While some part of her mind chastised her for caring one whit what Adam thought about her, another part yearned to confess all about her unhappy love affair with Jake Stark. But finally she decided it was too soon. She was normally such a private person, a friend could know her for years and never hear that story. The cozy, candlelit atmosphere, along with the vintage wine and fine food, encouraged the sharing of confidences, but Meredith knew she wasn't quite ready to bare her soul.

Meredith looked away from his open, caring expression. "Like I said, it was a long time ago...and not a subject I enjoy talking about. Besides, I'm still curious about you. Do you have any children?" she asked suddenly.

Why had that particular question popped into her mind? She wasn't sure. It seemed a good ploy to take the spotlight off her romantic past, however.

"No children," he replied, then sighed. "I certainly

regret that my marriage didn't last. But I regret not having any children even more."

"You're still young. It's not too late for you to have a family," she assured him.

Her words brightened his mood considerably, she noticed...but not in the way she'd hoped. "I'm glad you think so, Meredith. Maybe there's some hope here after all," he added. The gleam in his eye told the rest of the story. He believed her simple comment meant that she was sizing him up as marriage material.

The very thought was...absurd. Wasn't it? Meredith took a sip of ice water and coughed. Well, even if she had been floating along in fantasyland for a few moments, this latest news bulletin had surely brought her crashing down to earth.

Children. Of course.

He was definitely the family man type. He'd make a great father, too, she was sure. She guessed he was about forty, and plenty of men started families at that age and even later these days. She was sure he found no lack of women eager to fulfill his dream.

But he'd have to scratch her name off that list. Motherhood was simply not in the picture for her. Meredith could guarantee that.

She fantasized sometimes about having a baby. This was especially true when she was in the park, and she caught sight of some happy woman strolling a plump-cheeked baby or cradling a newborn to her chest in one of those cuddly baby pouches.

But in more rational moments the thought of motherhood scared her silly. She knew she'd be a disaster as a mother. It wasn't something you could learn out of a book. You had to feel it, deep inside, Meredith thought. She'd had such a poor example of marriage and mothering in her own life, Meredith was convinced she'd be totally incapable of raising a child, of providing the care and nurturing a child needed to thrive and grow into a happy, confident adult.

No, children were not in the picture for her. And just one more reason why this budding involvement with Adam just wouldn't work out.

Meredith sat quietly, sipping her coffee as she considered these sobering thoughts. "Anything wrong?" Adam asked. "I've been boring you silly with the story of my life, and you're too polite to admit it, right?'

She smiled and touched his hand. "Not at all. I still have an entire list of questions I want to ask you."

He seemed flattered. "The only thing I think I've left out so far is my blood type. What else could you possibly want to know about me?"

"Lots of things." She shrugged. "What's your middle name?"

He smiled. Deep dimples creased his cheeks as he modestly shook his head. "Can't tell. It's too embarrassing."

"It can't be worse than mine."

"Which is?"

She took a deep breath. "Agatha."

"Yes, that is bad," he agreed with a wince. "I guess I have to tell you mine, then. It's Sherman."

"Really? You don't look at all like a Sherman."

"Thank you. You don't look at all like an Agatha."

She laughed. "Maybe because my middle name is really Marie."

His eyes widened. "You tricked me?"

She grinned. "Yes, I guess I did."

And it was about time she got the edge on him, she thought proudly.

He sat back and shook his head. "I'll have to keep my eye on you."

"Yes, I guess you will...*Sherman.*"

It was a short taxi ride back to her apartment, and though Meredith tried to persuade Adam to let her off and keep the cab, he insisted on seeing her to the door.

Her fingers fumbled with the keys as she unlocked the outer door. She could feel him standing close behind her. Was he going to kiss her when she turned around? she wondered.

Should she invite him up? Considering what had happened Friday night on her living room couch, that idea was asking for disaster. Besides, it was late, and they both had to work tomorrow. How late was it? she suddenly wondered. She had been enjoying herself so much she had totally lost all track of time.

As she finally opened the door, she glanced down at her watch. "Goodness...poor Lucy. She must be dying to go out." Without waiting for Adam's response, she flew through the door and headed to the stairwell, taking the steps two at a time.

Adam followed closely behind her. She realized he must have thought she was just trying to avoid kissing him good-night. The truth was she had actually been looking forward to that part of the evening. More than she'd ever admit. But her concern for Lucy was sincere. The dog was not walked all day while Meredith was at work, and whenever she planned to stay out after work, she always arranged for either Lila, Sylvie or Rose to walk her. Her impromptu date with Adam had distracted her, and she'd forgotten all about poor Lucy.

Meredith quickly unlatched her front door, and Lucy bounded toward her out of the darkness with a happy yelp. Meredith grabbed the dog's leash and quickly clipped it to her collar.

"You're going to take her for a walk...now?" Adam asked. Meredith and Lucy flew by as the dog dragged her owner down the hallway.

"Of course. A nice long walk in the park. The poor thing has been cooped up all day."

The elevator doors stood open. Meredith and Lucy entered, and Adam leaped in just as the doors began to close. "But it's after eleven. You really can't walk around the park at this hour, Meredith. It's not safe," Adam said.

His stern, protective tone caught Meredith by surprise. She wasn't used to anyone looking after her...or telling her what she could and could not do.

"Don't be silly. We'll be fine," Meredith replied. The doors opened on the first floor, and they all got out, Lucy in the lead, straining at her leash.

"I can walk her for you. I'd love to," Adam insisted as they quickly crossed the lobby.

"Honestly, it's not at all necessary," Meredith replied. She opened the heavy door that led outside and kept a firm hold on Lucy as they descended the front steps. When they came to the sidewalk, Meredith kept a firm hold on Lucy's leash as the dog pulled her hopefully toward the entrance of the park across the street.

"Well...I guess you ought to wait here for a taxi," she said to Adam.

"No way," he insisted. "If you won't let me walk the dog, I'm going with you."

"Really, Adam—"

"I insist." She could tell from the firm, unyielding expression on his handsome face that there was no use arguing the point.

A few minutes later they were strolling in the moonlit park on one of Meredith's favorite trails that led to the lake. Lucy happily trotted along, sniffing every tree trunk. Meredith was glad that Adam didn't feel inclined to talking anymore. She breathed in the fresh autumn air and listened to the night sounds coming from all directions in the dark woods.

"The park is beautiful at night," Adam said quietly. "I'm glad I forced my company on you."

Meredith glanced up at him and smiled. "I am, too," she admitted. Then he slipped his arm around her shoulder and they fell into step together, and it seemed too perfect to spoil it by saying any more.

Finally they reached the lake. The dark waters were smooth as a mirror, and the sky was a canopy of stars overhead. Beyond the treetops, they could see the silvery skyline of the city's tallest buildings.

They sat on a bench at the lakeside. Adam pulled her close, and she relaxed against him, resting her head on his shoulder. She felt him kiss the top of her head and nuzzle his face in her hair.

She turned toward him, and his seeking mouth met hers. He cupped her face with his hand and kissed her deeply. Meredith answered his kiss, responding with a flood of longing for him. When his strong arms pulled her closer and his tongue dipped into her mouth, she felt herself melt into his embrace. They sat together kissing and holding each other for what seemed to Meredith a very long time.

Finally Adam lifted his head. He breathed deeply and squeezed her close, and she could tell he was struggling to control his desire for her. "Were you going to ask me up tonight?" he asked quietly.

She laughed. "I don't know...I wasn't sure," she answered honestly. "I mean, I wanted to...but..."

"You were afraid of what might happen," he finished for her.

She nodded, her forehead brushing his chest. He leaned back and lifted her chin so that she couldn't help but meet his dark, warm gaze.

"I wasn't going to come up, even if you asked me," he admitted. "Though saying no would have probably killed me. I want you so much. I wasn't sure I could control myself once we were alone," he admitted. "I don't want to give you any easy excuses to run away from me. I'll try to wait as long you want me to. But you're not going to get rid of me, Meredith. I don't want to lose you," he confided, his voice sounding suddenly full of emotion.

Meredith didn't know how to answer. All evening she'd been struggling to convince herself that she wasn't getting romantically involved with Adam. But it appeared he had a far different impression. And with good reason, she reflected. Who was she kidding? She was in too deep...way over her head.

"As I said earlier, I'll be out of town until the end of the week," he said. Thank heaven, she thought. She needed at least a week to cool off from these intense encounters. "Can I see you on Saturday night? I have to attend an opening reception at the museum, here in the park. It's not terribly formal. It should be fun, especially with you," he suggested.

"I'd love to go," Meredith said sincerely.

She often visited the museum, but had never attended an opening there. She guessed that Adam made large donations to the organization in order to be invited to such exclusive events. He was active in so many charitable, civic-minded causes and clearly wanted to use his wealth and influence to help others. She admired that quality in him. The more she got to know him, in fact, the more she found to admire and the more he contradicted her stereotyped ideas about wealthy, successful men.

They sat quietly, looking out at the lake and the starry sky. It felt so warm and comfortable in the shelter of his embrace, Meredith didn't want to move. Finally she said, "I guess we ought to go back."

Adam nodded. "I guess so," he said.

Still, he moved away from her slowly, reluctantly, softly kissing her a few more times as he gradually let go. As if he'd hoped they could stay just that way, sitting together until sunrise. She understood how he felt. She felt exactly the same.

They both stood up. Meredith's legs felt like rubber and she forced herself to come back down to earth. For some reason, Lucy remained lying down next to the bench, where she had settled some time ago. She looked up at Meredith expectantly.

"That's a well-trained dog," Adam observed with a wry smile. "She was so considerate about not... interrupting us."

"Yes, she was." Meredith couldn't quite understand it. "You weren't slipping her dog biscuits, were you?"

"No...but I will keep that trick in mind for next time," Adam promised. He took hold of Meredith's hand and twined his long fingers through hers as they started to walk home.

Meredith laughed, but inside she trembled with breathless anticipation. He had promised to be patient. Yet, Adam had also promised that he wouldn't let her get away from him. She had to give him some credit there. Clearly a good judge of character, he already anticipated the emotional roadblocks she might throw in his way. She knew now that when the time came, she wouldn't escape his passionate embrace quite as easily as she had tonight.

The truth was, Meredith knew she wouldn't even want to….

Six

"Wow, who sent the roses?" Sylvie asked as she peeked into Meredith's office on Tuesday morning.

The huge arrangement of long-stemmed roses on her desk was hard to ignore, and of course Sylvie would want to know all the details, Meredith realized.

"Just...a client," Meredith replied. She tried to suppress the smile that came automatically to her lips every time she thought of Adam, but she just couldn't. The roses had arrived early that morning with a card that said, "Missing you already, Adam." She had slipped the card in her purse for safekeeping and now glanced at Sylvie, then looked away.

For some reason she felt shy telling anyone about what had been going on between herself and Adam. Even Sylvie. But Sylvie knew her so well by now, the look on Meredith's face and the gleam in her eyes probably gave everything away. Still, Meredith attempted to change the subject.

"Did I miss anything important at the production meeting this morning?"

With her work on the Everlasting samples and Adam's account, her boss had excused her from the meeting. Meredith had been grateful.

Sylvie took her usual seat beside Meredith's drawing table and crossed her long slim legs. "No real news. A tentative production schedule was set for the Everlasting Collection, but I'm sure Frank will fill you in." Sylvie stared at her in a way that made Meredith realize she wasn't letting her off the hook. "So is there any connection between you coming in late this morning and the portable greenhouse?"

"Maybe," Meredith admitted.

"And is this 'just a client' the same 'just a client' who sent that beautiful sweater set last week?" Sylvie continued.

Meredith's gaze flew up to meet her friend's. "Honestly, Sylvie. You should open a detective agency. You're really good."

Sylvie shrugged and leaned closer. "It's Adam Richards, right? He was the one who bought you at the auction, and Jayne said she called you to consult with him down in the showroom last week. I didn't get to see him at the auction, but Jayne says he's gorgeous. Why didn't you tell us that you're seeing him?"

Meredith sat back, wide-eyed. "For goodness sakes, yes, he did buy me at the auction, but all we did afterward was have coffee, and since then all we've done is have dinner. A business dinner," she added. "Honestly, nothing has happened," she insisted. But the look on Sylvie's face made it hard for Meredith to get away with her little white lie. ''Well...practically nothing. I mean, nothing happened that most other people would really think was anything.... But of course, since I don't really date much—I mean, I don't date at all, actually—I mean, to me it seemed like something. Even though it really was absolutely—''

''Meredith, you're babbling,'' Sylvie gently interrupted. ''You really like this guy, don't you?''

''Yeah...I really do,'' Meredith admitted. ''And it scares me to death, Sylvie,'' she added, looking up at the roses. ''He's just so...so...''

''Perfect?'' Sylvie asked.

''He's too perfect,'' Meredith replied with a sigh. ''He's intelligent, kind, considerate... He even told me last night he's not going to give me any excuses to get away from him. I think he really means it.''

''Sounds like he already knows you pretty well,'' Sylvie said with a laugh. ''But if he's so great, why would you want to get away? Maybe this could be it.''

''You have an optimistic view about romance. I wish I could be more like you, I really do. But I just don't have any luck picking men. No matter how great it seems at first, it just doesn't work out for me.''

Sylvie stared at Meredith with an expression of concern and sympathy. Wisely, she didn't offer any further advice or ask any more prying questions but simply reached over Meredith's desk and patted her hand. Meredith wasn't close to many people, but at that moment she deeply appreciated Sylvie's friendship.

''Are you going to see him again?''

Meredith nodded. ''He's taking me to a reception at the Bentley Museum on Saturday night. It's a cocktail party for big donors.''

Sylvie looked impressed. "Wow, you can't miss that date. What are you going to wear?"

Meredith suddenly looked at her. "Gee—I haven't even thought about it. He said it's not formal. But what does that mean, coming from a millionaire?"

After a brief discussion of Meredith's wardrobe, the two women decided to go shopping on Thursday night. Sylvie had such a good fashion sense, Meredith was grateful she would have her opinion in the dressing room.

"So...after Saturday you're not going to see him anymore, is that what you're thinking?"

Meredith rose from her chair and paced across her small office. "I just don't know. I don't know what to do."

Sylvie rose, too, and gave Meredith a sympathetic look. "Why don't you just relax...and take it one step at a time? You'll figure it out," she assured her.

"At least one of us trusts my instincts about men."

"Just trust your heart, Meredith," Sylvie advised with a small smile.

Sylvie then changed the subject and talked about the auction. It had been the most successful one to date and she felt the event had really helped rally the Colette employees. Meredith had to agree and was glad now that her friends had persuaded her to take part.

After Sylvie had gone, Meredith was left alone with her roses to ponder the wisdom of her friend's advice.

Meredith did not expect Adam to call her while he was away, but she couldn't help missing him. His image was never far from her thoughts all week, and at night she lay in bed unable to fall asleep, with a whirlwind of questions spinning through her head.

On Friday night she had gone to bed early, and the ringing phone at her bedside woke her. She glanced at the clock. It was nearly midnight. The only person she could imagine calling at that hour was her mother, who could never quite remember that in California it was two hours earlier than in the Midwest.

"Hello?" Meredith answered groggily.

"Did I wake you? I'm sorry. I just got in and I wanted to hear your voice."

It was Adam. The sound of his voice woke her instantly. She sat up in bed and smiled. "I'm glad you called. How was your trip?"

"Exhausting. But I got a lot done." He shared a few details about his business activities and the various problems he'd encountered. Meredith was pleased that he felt free to confide in her. "I'm beat...but I just wanted to say hello."

Meredith cupped the phone to her ear. She wished he was sitting right beside her. "Hello," she said softly.

He breathed out a long sigh. "I missed you."

"I missed you, too," she admitted. "Thank you for the roses," she thought to add, "they're beautiful."

"I'm glad they pleased you. Four days can be a long time. I didn't want you to forget me."

She laughed. As if she ever could. "Good idea. I think it worked," she teased him.

"We're still getting together tomorrow night?" he asked. His deep voice sounded as confident as ever, yet Meredith thought she detected the slightest questioning note. As if he half expected her to make some excuse and stand him up.

"Yes, of course. I haven't forgotten that, either," she promised him.

"Good," he said quietly. His voice sounded so warm

and pleased, she could imagine the light in his dark eyes. They chatted some more and arranged a time for Adam to pick her up.

"Well, good night," he said finally. "Sweet dreams."

Her dreams would be much sweeter now, she thought, though she didn't dare admit it. "Good night, Adam," she whispered as she hung up the phone.

Just before Adam was to pick her up on Saturday night, Meredith surveyed herself in the full-length bedroom mirror. Good thing she'd given Sylvie free rein the other night during their shopping expedition. Meredith would never have thought to try on the little suit. The sheath-style dress was short and fitted with a rounded neckline. It displayed her perfect figure and long legs in a manner that Sylvie promised was "totally classy." The matching fitted coat had long lapels and a single button. Sylvie had convinced her that the ensemble was perfect for the occasion—stylish, not too dressy and definitely on the arty side with the right jewelry. Meredith had chosen abstract-shaped gold earrings she'd fashioned herself, and at the last minute decided to fasten Rose's unique brooch to the shoulder of her coat, which kept the black fabric from looking too stark, she thought.

She'd decided to wear her hair down, parted on the side with a hunk of the thick curls held back by a comb. Sylvie had also strong-armed her into a stop at the cosmetics counter, and Meredith had compromised on a tube of mascara, some eye shadow and lip color.

The saleswoman had been surprisingly understanding about Meredith's aversion to makeup—much more than Sylvie was, actually. She had shown her how to apply the makeup sparingly but quite effectively, to achieve a natural look with which Meredith felt quite comfortable.

As she slipped on a pair of black pumps, she wondered why she'd gone to such trouble. To soothe her own anxieties about not being "pretty" enough for Adam? That wasn't a very good reason—Adam had always assured her he liked her just the way she was. Maybe her efforts would only be icing on the cake, Meredith hoped.

Moments later, when Meredith opened the door to greet him, the look on his face told her exactly why she'd gone to such lengths.

"Wow, you look gorgeous," he said, meeting her gaze with an intense, dark look. "How am I supposed to enjoy the artwork tonight? I'll be too distracted by you."

"Don't be silly," Meredith said as he helped her on with her coat. But his compliments did make her feel lighthearted and very attractive, and she practically floated down to Adam's car.

The museum looked dazzling at night, Meredith thought. The building's architectural design was a mixture of thoroughly modern lines and the classic proportions of Greek or Roman antiquity. The large entrance was decorated with brightly colored banners announcing the new exhibit, and brilliant outdoor lights emphasized the building's large scale and dramatic lines. She felt as if she was entering a castle.

Looking perfectly suited to the setting, a crowd of elegantly dressed men and women mingled in the vast lobby, sipping champagne. Meredith felt suddenly nervous and ill at ease. She disliked parties, even when she knew most of the other guests. This gathering was quite intimidating to her. Adam seemed to sense her sudden wave of nervousness immediately and took her hand, twining their fingers together.

"Don't worry, Meredith, this is going to be fun," he whispered in her ear. "There are a few people here I really want you to meet. People who can help you with your career. Nobody will bite you, I promise," he teased her.

She turned and laughed at him, feeling her shyness subside. "Adam, don't be silly."

"Present company excluded, of course," he added with a sly grin. "But we'll get to that later."

Meredith glanced up at the tall, commanding figure beside her and felt an all-too-familiar sense of attraction and desire. This evening promised to be more than their first time socializing as a couple, she realized. Were they a "couple" she wondered? Things were moving so fast. If she wasn't careful, she'd soon be Adam's lover. Whether or not he'd promised to wait forever for that step....

"Adam, good to see you." An attractive, fair-haired man broke away from the group he was talking to and approached Adam with a wide smile. His long, blond hair nearly touched his collar and curled slightly at the ends. He held out his hand, and Adam took it eagerly in his own.

The first thing Meredith noticed about him, aside from his good looks, was his outfit. His gray-blue jacket was made of an iridescent-looking fabric. Underneath, he wore a tailored silk shirt of exactly the same hue. He wore no tie, and the shirt was buttoned to the very top. The jacket and shirt looked quite expensive, she thought, perhaps from an Italian or French designer's shop. His tight black jeans and black Western boots seemed an incongruent match, but somehow it all worked.

"David, good to see you. I was hoping I'd run into you here," Adam greeted him. "This is David Martin,

Meredith. He owns the Pendleton–Martin gallery on Pace Street,'' Adam added, naming the well-known avenue at the center of the city's art district.

''How do you do, Meredith?'' David said, extending his hand.

Meredith shook his hand briefly. ''Nice to meet you,'' she said.

''And by the way, I just own the Martin half,'' David clarified with a charming laugh. ''My partner, Tom Pendleton, would hate it if I took all the credit.''

''Well, you're the one who curates the exhibits, as I understand it,'' Adam said. ''Meredith is a very talented artist. A sculptor, actually. You ought to take a look at her work. She's terrific, honestly.''

Meredith could barely believe what she'd just heard. Why hadn't Adam warned her about introducing a gallery owner? She was grateful…yet felt as if the rug had just been pulled right out from under her feet. In one part of her mind, a huge neon sign flashed, reading, Big Break! but when David looked her way, Meredith felt her throat grow dry.

''There's a great demand for sculpture lately. All these Wall Street whiz kids need to fill up their lofts and mansions,'' he joked. ''And we're always on the lookout for new talent,'' he said encouragingly. ''Are you with any other gallery right now, Meredith?''

''Uh…no. No, I'm not. I've been in some group shows over the past few years,'' she stammered. ''But I'm really a jewelry designer…I mean, that's how I earn my living.''

David just smiled—an indulgent one, she thought. Darn, she'd blown it.

''I work in metal mostly. Right now I'm working on

some very large pieces, using found objects and different types of metal,'' she added hurriedly.

''That sounds interesting,'' David replied. He did seem interested, she thought. Or was he just being polite? ''Where do you assemble these pieces?''

''I have a studio on State Street, in a warehouse.''

''Can I come by there sometime? Or maybe you could send some slides?'' he suggested.

''Sure. I mean, either would be fine.''

''We have a group show coming up in December. Perhaps something of yours would fit in. Give me call.''

He offered Meredith his card along with another friendly smile. ''Thanks very much,'' she replied.

''If she doesn't call, I will,'' Adam promised.

David laughed and glanced from Adam back to Meredith. That's the way people look at you when you're really a couple, she thought.

''If I do take her on, you may have to get a percentage as her agent, Adam,'' David joked.

''Just a dedicated fan.'' Adam glanced admiringly at Meredith, and she felt her cheeks grow even warmer.

''Yes, I'm sure,'' David said, glancing back at her. ''Nice to meet you. Enjoy the show.''

After David drifted off, Meredith still felt a bit stunned. The owner of a well-known art gallery had actually offered to see her work. How could that have happened so easily? She looked up to find Adam watching her, trying to read the expression on her face and looking a bit puzzled, she thought.

Adam could make things happen with the snap of his fingers. He knew important people; he had influence. Was it right to trade off his influence, though? she wondered.

"Are you mad at me for springing David on you?" he asked.

"He did offer to see my work, so I guess I'd be awfully ungrateful to be angry with you," she said.

Adam laughed. "I did consider giving you some warning," he admitted. "But I wasn't even sure he'd be here, and I didn't want to get your hopes up for nothing."

"Or get me so rattled I'd stand you up?" she added with a wry smile.

"Well...that possibility did cross my mind," he admitted.

She probably should have been mad at him, but with his dark good looks and brilliant smile, he was simply too handsome to stay mad at for very long.

He rested his hands on her shoulders and stared down at her. "I just wanted to help you a little. Still, that doesn't mean I'd ever want you to be any other way, Meredith," he promised her in a sultry whisper.

"I know," she assured him.

He gazed at her for a long moment, seeming very satisfied with her reply. "Let's see the show, shall we?" he suggested. Taking her arm, he led her to the first gallery.

Adam seemed to know just about everyone there and David wasn't the only acquaintance to which she was introduced. At first she felt her old shyness rising up, but Adam's solid, poised presence beside her and the firm touch of his hand on her back gave her confidence, as if she was absorbing the warmth of a steadily growing fire. He made her feel at ease and self-assured—even with these wealthy, prestigious strangers—by introducing her with an unmistakable note of pride and affection in his voice.

As Meredith had suspected, there were many single women at the gathering who sought out Adam. He chatted in a pleasant, friendly way with each of them. But Meredith was relieved to notice that none of his admirers seemed able to bring that certain, special light to his dark eyes. The light she saw each time he looked her way.

After viewing the artwork, they decided to have dinner at a small café in the area, a few blocks from Meredith's apartment. It was one of Meredith's favorites, and the intimate, quiet setting was a perfect atmosphere to discuss the exhibit. But all the while they chatted about the artwork and other topics, the wheels in Meredith's mind spun. It would have been a perfect evening…if only she wasn't so nervous about how it would end.

Staring across the table at Adam's strong, chiseled features and warm-brown eyes, she had never before felt more attracted to a man. Yet, the intensity of her attraction and desire was matched by her fear of falling in love and eventually finding herself with a broken heart.

Suddenly Meredith worried Adam would think she was beholden to him in some way for his introduction to the gallery owner. She knew rationally that he didn't think like that, but irrationally, she couldn't help worrying…and wanting to set things straight.

Impulsively she said, "Adam, I want to thank you again for introducing me to David Martin. You've seen so little of my artwork. It was very generous of you to put your opinion on the line like that."

"Nonsense." He covered her hand with his. "You don't have to thank me. You're immensely talented, Meredith. David is the one who should be grateful. I'm sure he'll love your work."

"Well…whatever happens, I appreciate the favor,"

she said, sounding a bit formal, she thought, even to her own ears. "But I hope you're not under the impression that this...changes our relationship in any way?"

He lifted his head, his eyes widening in surprise. "Changes our relationship? How do you mean?"

Now she really felt put on the spot and suddenly regretted even bringing up the subject. "Oh...forget it," she said, shaking her head.

"No, I want to know what you mean. How do you think it will change our relationship?" he persisted.

Did he sound annoyed...or even angry? She wasn't sure. He sounded determined not to let the subject drop, that much she was certain of. She took a deep breath and looked back up at him, meeting his dark gaze head-on.

"I was just worried that you might feel that I'm... obliged to you in some way for the favor. That's all," she admitted.

He laughed, a short, harsh sound. "Meredith, you don't know me very well, do you? I don't need to trade on favors with women for sex, if that's what you're driving at."

Meredith suddenly felt ashamed for seeming to accuse him of such motives. "I'm sorry," she stammered. "That's not quite what I meant. Honestly."

He sighed. She could see his expression soften as he gazed at her, though she sensed that he was still hurt and unhappy by her accusation. "What *did* you mean, then?" he asked.

"I'm afraid," she admitted. "Afraid that we're getting too...involved."

There, she'd said it. Things hadn't yet gone that far. But tonight was a turning point, for better or worse. Maybe she could get out with her heart intact after all.

He sat back and stared at her. She could see that her words had hurt him, and she felt an echoing pang in her own heart. But just as quickly his expression changed to a bland, unreadable mask.

"To the contrary, I don't feel that way at all. I mean, I enjoy your company, Meredith. You know that. But if you want to keep things strictly...platonic between us, it's okay. I can handle it," he promised her. "I just appreciate having a date now and again. You've been a great help fending off all the aggressive females that usually home in on me when I attend one of these events alone. That's the only trade-off I expect," he added.

His words and the cool, offhand tone of his delivery stung her deeply. Was that all she meant to him? A decoy to discourage other women? For a moment she felt as if she couldn't breathe. She knew that having a man like Adam interested in her was really too good to be true. When she looked up at him again, the right words wouldn't come, and she felt her eyes fill with hot tears.

"Well, if that's the real reason you asked me out, I think it's time for this decoy to call it a night." Rising from her chair, she grabbed her purse. "Goodbye, Adam," she mumbled through her tears. She turned and fled.

"Meredith...wait," she heard him call after her. But she knew he had to stop to pay the bill and hoped that task would prevent him from catching up.

Out on the street, the air was brisk. She thought to hail a cab, but then realized that she was only a few short blocks from home. Hoping to escape Adam's pursuit, she started off at a brisk pace, nearly running down the street.

She soon turned the corner on Amber Court, and her

building came into sight. She unlocked the outer door and let herself in. She didn't even bother to check her mail but went straight up to her apartment. As she reached her door and took out her keys again, she felt relieved that she had asked Sylvie to give Lucy her evening walk. At least she didn't have to go outside again and risk meeting Adam.

But just as she was putting her key into the lock, she heard heavy footsteps in the stairwell, and Adam appeared at the end of the hall.

She turned, shocked to see him, then realized that in her rush, she must have left the outer door ajar and that's how he'd gotten in.

"Meredith, please wait," Adam called out as he walked quickly toward her.

She looked at him, then turned away, facing the door. She whisked her fingertips under her tear-soaked eyes, cursing the fact that tonight of all nights, she'd worn eye makeup. How ironic. On top of everything, I must look like a raccoon, she thought.

"Meredith, please..." She heard his voice close behind her but didn't turn around. "I really need to talk to you."

She turned and faced him. "Haven't you said enough already?"

"Please, let me explain. Then I'll go...I promise."

The naked, pleading look on his face was her undoing. Besides, she didn't feel like causing a scene out in the hallway so late at night. She felt she had no choice but to speak to him. For the last time, she hoped.

"All right...come inside," she said with a long sigh.

Seven

They went inside and Meredith closed the door. She took a few steps into the apartment and dropped her purse and keys on a small hall table. She unbuttoned her coat but didn't take it off. She turned to see Adam still standing by the door.

"Okay, say what you have to say, then go, please," she told him curtly.

"Meredith, please. Just listen to me for a second." He was still a bit winded from chasing her all the way from the café, then running up the stairs. He held up his hands, as if to frame her face, but didn't dare to touch her. "I lied to you just now. What I said, about wanting your company just to discourage other women…that wasn't true. Not at all," he said in a rush.

"Oh?" Meredith tilted her head to one side. "How do I know you're telling me the truth now?"

"Because you know in your heart, I'm not a liar," he

said, moving toward her. "I'd never lie to you, in fact. Except that I know how hesitant you are about getting close to me. And how frightened you are of your own feelings for me."

His observations were right on target and, put so bluntly, his words forced Meredith to pull her gaze away from his knowing eyes.

"I thought I'd make up some handy excuse that would put you at ease so you wouldn't feel so threatened. I was desperate, I guess. Scared out of my wits that you were trying to stop seeing me...isn't that true?"

She nodded and sighed. A strand of hair fell across her eyes, and she brushed it back with her hand. "You've got me figured out to a T," she admitted.

So, Adam did feel deeply about her, after all. Is that what he was saying? Meredith's emotions were running so high her head was spinning. She looked up at him, and he slipped his arms around her. When he pulled her close, she didn't resist. She circled his waist with her arms and rested her head on his broad chest.

"I couldn't stand the idea of not seeing you anymore," he whispered in a rough voice. "I'm just so...crazy about you. Please forgive me for lying to you like that. I never meant to hurt your feelings. You believe me, don't you?"

His voice was so emotional and sincere, how could she not? In her heart she knew his words were true. And she felt as if she'd just been struck by lightning, realizing how much Adam truly cared for her. She leaned back and looked up at him. "Of course I believe you," she assured him. "I'm sorry, too...for doubting you and... running away from you."

"I told you once before, Meredith, I'm not going to

let you get away from me.'' His low, seductive tone set every nerve ending smoldering.

''Now you've proved it,'' she observed.

''I'll prove it again and again, if necessary.''

Would it be necessary? Meredith wondered. She willed herself to move away from him but simply couldn't. It felt so good, being held close this way and holding him in return. Too good to give up. He bent his head to kiss her, and she lifted her mouth to meet his searching lips. She felt complete, connected, cherished and desired. Her days of running from him were over. She was ready to surrender to the conclusion that now seemed inevitable from the very start.

Their kisses deepened, Adam's touch turning possessive and passionate as he slipped Meredith's coat off her arms and it dropped in a heap at her feet. He pulled away from her for an instant to quickly pull off his own coat and jacket. Then his arms were around her again, his mouth merging and melting against her own. His warm touch glided up and down her back, following the rich curves of her body, her small waist and the flair of hips and thighs. Meredith felt his fingers at the top of the zipper that ran down her back, then suddenly a gust of air cooled her bare skin as the zipper dropped to her waist. With a tender, seductive touch, Adam's warm mouth followed the curve of her arched neck and covered her shoulders with soft kisses. He deftly slipped the dress off her shoulders, and it, too, dropped to the floor around her feet, revealing the lace-trimmed black silk slip that she wore underneath.

Adam pulled his head away from her for a moment and took her in from head to toe. She heard his sharp intake of breath, and the unmistakable flash of arousal in his eyes lit fires deep within her.

"God...you are absolutely gorgeous," he whispered hoarsely, pulling her close again. "Absolutely," he repeated, just as their mouths met again in a hungry kiss.

His hands slipped over her slim hips to cup her bottom as he pulled her close to the heat of his body. Pressed so intimately against him, Meredith could not mistake his need for her. She kissed him back, wildly, passionately, desperately. As if a dam of longing inside her had suddenly burst. Her hands moved eagerly over his taut body, caressing the hard muscles of his shoulders and broad back, then dropping lower to his waist. She slipped her hands between them to loosen his tie and unfasten the buttons of his shirt. As she peeled his shirt away, she kissed the strong column of his neck, then moved her mouth lower, to cover his bare chest with soft kisses. As her tongue playfully circled his flat masculine nipples, she heard him groan, and his hold on her grew so tight she could barely breathe. "Meredith... you're driving me wild," he gasped.

He pulled back for an instant and stared at her, a look so heated and intense it stole Meredith's breath. He took her hand and led her to the bedroom and Meredith silently followed.

Moments later they were once again wrapped in each other's arms, stretched out on Meredith's queen-size bed.

His lips met hers, warm and persuasive, questioning and receiving her unspoken reply. With a heartfelt sigh of surrender, Meredith pressed her long, slim body against Adam's hard length. Her legs intimately entwined with his as she opened her mouth to his enticing assault. Their tongues twined and merged in a hot, wet foray, and Meredith felt Adam's strong hands first in her hair, then sweeping over her body, stroking and caressing her, molding and exploring her. His hot mouth moved lower, down the smooth line of her neck, to her collarbone and then to her full throbbing breasts. His lips covered the thin, silky fabric, teasing her nipple to a taut tingling peak. Meredith's breath caught in her throat, her hands gripping his shoulders as waves of sensual pleasure swept through her limbs.

"God, you're so beautiful," Adam groaned against her skin as his hands deftly smoothed down the straps of her slip. She felt a cool shock of air on her bare skin for a moment, quickly replaced by Adam's warm mouth. As his tongue and lips drew her to even higher heights, his hand glided up her thigh, then up and under her slip to cup her bottom. He eased off her panty hose and bikini underwear and Meredith arched against him, emitting a soulful sigh of satisfaction as his probing fingers explored even further, seeking and finding the source of her wet, warm womanhood. An ache of longing built inside of her, powerful and even painful in its intensity—a yearning chasm that could only be satisfied by a total union with the man who now pleasured her body so thoroughly, so effortlessly, drawing her to him, body and soul.

Their tongues twined together in a deep, soulful kiss as his hands skimmed over her waist, finally coming to rest on her slim hips. Suddenly she was shocked into awareness as he lifted her up against him, his mouth moving hungrily against her own. She felt the hard, throbbing evidence of his arousal under his trousers and stroked him with her hand.

He pulled his head back, his chest rising against hers as he dragged in a deep breath of air. "I want you so much, Meredith...if you need me to stop, you'll have to say so now,'' he urged her as his head turned toward her on the pillow they shared.

She met his gaze in the dark. ''I want to make love with you, Adam...I've never wanted anything more,'' she whispered. She kissed him hard on the lips as her hands eagerly unfastened his pants and then pulled them down his hips. He reached up and covered her breasts with his hands. He sighed against her mouth, a totally intoxicating sound that communicated an unspoken message of admiration and pure delight in touching her...and being touched by her. Emboldened by his reaction, Meredith pulled back slightly, then slipped a trembling hand into the waistband of his briefs. He felt hard and hot against her hand, pulsing with need as her seductive touch first teased, then thoroughly satisfied him. Adam kissed her fervently, his swift, intense response almost frightening to her. He moved away for a moment, quickly slipping off his briefs, then moved back and pulled her into his arms.

He moved over her, covering her body with his own. He lifted his head and stared deeply into her eyes. Moonlight filtered into the room through the half-opened curtain, casting his rugged features and powerful expression in a luminous light. His eyes looked black, like polished black jewels, she thought, a tempest of passion swirling in their depths.

Then he shifted, his hips fitting between her thighs. He pulled her close and moved inside of her in a swift, hard stroke.

She trembled with pleasure at the shock of their joining. Her head nestled against his shoulder, and her fingers dug into the bunched muscles of his arms. She heard him expel a long, harsh breath, a sigh of deeply felt pleasure as he began to move inside her, slowly at first, as he described his own deeply felt pleasure in soft, thrilling whispers.

Then Meredith felt her hips rock against his in perfect rhythm, matching him sigh for sigh. Adam filled her, completed her, unlike any encounter with her first lover, Jake. Adam was an expert lover, striving to pleasure her with every ounce of his body and soul. She yearned for the dazzling heat and light to last forever, and though she felt she could barely stand it anymore, he urged her on even higher, her pleasure rising to unimagined peaks.

Meredith was barely aware as Adam moved above her. He lifted himself up on his arms, over her. With her long legs wrapped tightly about his waist, their rhythm grew stronger, harder and even more intense. He moved deeper and deeper with every thrust, satisfying her more completely than she ever dreamed possible. As she moved as one with him, as close as any two people could be, Meredith felt her body and soul open to him, in complete and utter surrender.

She was letting it all go—the futile battle to keep him away, physically and emotionally. Now she could see that her struggles had been useless—a waste of time, really. He'd had her heart from the first, that first dark gaze and heart-stopping smile. Her hands glided sensually down his powerful body, her heart and mind overwhelmed by the wonder of her feelings for him. She felt her body tighten around him, exploding with pleasure in the pinnacle of ecstasy. She felt shattered, bursting into sparkling bits as she gripped him and shouted his name. He continued to move inside of her, and she urged him on to his own peak until, moments later, he arched against her and called out her name. His big body shook in her arms. The sheer wonder in his voice as he whispered her name again made her heart sing.

* * *

When Meredith woke, she wasn't sure how much time had passed, a few minutes or hours. Her head rested on Adam's broad chest, and she couldn't see his face. His breathing was slow and deep and she wondered if he was asleep. But when she felt his fingertips drifting gently through her hair, she knew he, too, was awake. Still, she didn't stir, feeling as if she didn't want to break the spell. In Adam's embrace she felt so content, desired and appreciated. She felt possessed and protected. Not in a smothering sense, but in a truly caring and totally sexy way. While making love, she had felt a sense of complete connection to Adam that she had never really felt with Jake Stark. Yet, she wondered if the encounter had been nearly as satisfying for Adam. After all, he was clearly a man with unlimited experience with women, while she had only had one other lover before him. Jake had known she was a virgin when he took her to bed and therefore had had no expectations. But maybe she should have warned Adam about her dire lack of experience. Perhaps he'd expected something…different and now he was disappointed.

She lifted her head and glanced up at him, trying to read the expression on his handsome face. His eyes had been closed, but they opened immediately, as if he sensed he was being looked at.

He smiled a wide, warm smile that creased the tiny lines at the corners of his eyes and created deep dimples in his lean cheeks. He was so very attractive to her. Somehow, even though they'd already made love for hours, she desired him even more.

"What's up?" he asked in a soft voice.

"Hmm, nothing," she said, resting her head on his chest once more.

"I can tell when something's bothering you by now, sweetheart," he replied. She felt the vibrations of his soft laugh against her cheek. "Come on, you can tell me. Are you having second thoughts about us making love?"

"No...not at all," she assured him. She lifted her head and propped her chin on her hand. "Are you?"

He looked surprised by her question. "Not at all. Why, did you think I might?"

"Not second thoughts, exactly..." She took a breath and pulled the sheet up a bit to cover her bare breasts. "It's just that you're such a great lover and clearly...so experienced...and I'm not," she admitted in a near whisper. "It couldn't have been very good for you."

He sat up, looking alarmed at her assumption. "Meredith, darling, don't be silly." When she wouldn't look up at him, he slid down beside her and took her face in his hands. He stared deeply into her wide, blue eyes. "Making love with you was fantastic. You're incredibly sexy, unbelievably gorgeous and totally giving. You're perfect in every way," he added, kissing her quickly on the mouth. "How could you ever think otherwise?" His dark brows drew together and he frowned. "Did some jerk, way back when, make you feel otherwise, Meredith?" he asked with concern.

"I've only had one lover before you, Adam. Back in college. The man I mentioned to you the other night," she added. "I will say the relationship didn't do much for my self-esteem," she admitted with a sigh.

He gazed down at her and brushed a curl of hair from her brow with his fingertips, then tenderly traced the line of her cheek. "Tell me something about him. Why didn't it work out?"

Meredith didn't like talking about Jake; especially

now, when she felt so close to Adam. She was not in the mood to summon up the shadows of her unhappy romantic past. But Adam's interest was genuine, and she knew it was important for him to know about her past romances, as she wanted to know all about his.

She told him the story of her affair with the older, sophisticated artist in as brief a version as she could manage. It was difficult when she reached the part about Jake's abrupt departure for New York and his curt rejection and how she later learned he'd been having affairs with at least two other students at the same time he'd been seeing her.

Adam's expression grew pale and taut. "What a predatory louse. A man like that should be too ashamed to live. He doesn't deserve to—" He cut himself off abruptly and shook his head. Then he pulled her close again and kissed her. "I wish I'd known you back then." He sighed. "At least I have you now. I feel so honored that after all this time, you chose to be with me," he confessed in a tender voice. "You're a very, very special woman, Meredith. I won't let you down," he promised.

Meredith felt too moved to answer him. Her arms surrounded his strong, solid body as he drew her closer to him. They slid down under the sheets again, expressing their feelings in a deep, soulful kiss. She could feel Adam's strong body ready to merge with hers again, and she was eager to receive him.

Despite her fears of becoming intimately involved with Adam, somehow she knew he would never intentionally hurt her, not the way Jake had done. But since their relationship was now taking a serious turn, she wondered if she would eventually be the one to disappoint him.

* * *

Meredith and Adam woke up late and took a long time before leaving her bed to face the outside world. If it hadn't been for poor Lucy, Meredith wondered if they would have left her bedroom at all. But finally, showered and dressed, they took a long walk in the park and had brunch.

The rest of the day passed in a blissful haze. Adam was very interested in seeing her studio, and since she needed to take care of some errands there, they drove over to the far side of the city. His praise for her completed sculptures and works in progress lifted Meredith's mood even more—if that were possible—and once again Adam reminded her to contact David Martin.

Their perfect day together finally ended at Adam's place, where he cooked a light dinner for them. Meredith had never suspected that he enjoyed working in the kitchen. He laughed out loud to learn that she could barely cook an egg. While Adam got their dinner ready, she looked over his private domain. The spacious, modern apartment was on the twenty-fifth floor of a luxury condo tower in one of the city's most prestigious neighborhoods. It was decorated with style, she thought, and soon learned that all of the furnishings were from his company.

Although Meredith had fully intended to return here right after supper, it seemed hard to leave Adam's side, especially once he began kissing her goodbye. Somehow she was persuaded to stay the night and woke up extra early in order to stop at her apartment first to drop off Lucy, shower and change, before dashing off to work.

After their weekend together, Meredith and Adam found it hard to be apart and saw each other nearly every night of the week. As one of the city's most prominent businessmen and a generous philanthropist, Adam's desk was stacked with invitations to fund-raising affairs and cocktail parties. Whenever he felt compelled to attend, he always asked Meredith to join him. At first she only agreed for Adam's sake—he always sounded as if he couldn't survive the evening if she didn't come along.

After the first few events, she almost found herself enjoying the experience of meeting new people and discussing interesting ideas and events. She knew that at Adam's side, she'd quickly gained poise and social skills. It was hard to believe, but she hardly ever felt the smothering blanket of shyness anymore, the annoying affliction that had plagued her for so long.

Her sharp-eyed pals, Sylvie, Lila and Jayne, were the first to notice the bloom in Meredith's cheeks and the spring in her step. After spending the weekend with Adam, Meredith finally felt confident enough about their relationship to tell her friends all about him. They agreed to meet for lunch at J.J.'s Deli, a favorite eatery for Colette employees. Meredith loved the overstuffed sandwiches and big sour pickles, and rarely turned down an invitation to meet her friends there. Even when she knew—like today—that she was going to get the third degree. But she told them all about Adam and patiently answered all their questions. Well, almost all of them.

Her friends were thrilled to hear that things were working out so well, and they laughingly congratulated themselves on doing such a magnificent job, dressing Meredith up for the auction.

Whenever Meredith now thought of the night of the auction, it seemed like such a long time ago, though it had been little more than two weeks. One evening, while clearing up the dresser top in her bedroom, Meredith discovered that she had never returned the brooch Rose had loaned her. She immediately went downstairs and knocked on Rose's door. Rose was happy to see her and wondered where she'd been hiding herself lately.

Meredith soon found herself sitting on Rose's sofa, holding a cup of soothing peppermint tea. She always loved being in Rose's spacious, airy apartment. Rose had wonderful taste, she thought, and a truly artistic eye for decorating. The walls were pure white, emphasizing the richly detailed antique moldings around the ceilings and doorways. The white background also showcased Rose's wonderful collection of sculpture and paintings. The furnishings also qualified as works of art, Meredith thought, and appeared to be genuine antiques, from both America and Europe. Yet, despite the many valuable treasures in Rose's home, the overall effect was one of comfort and timeless beauty. Rose's living room was one of the most relaxing places Meredith had ever found, and also a place that made it easy to open one's heart and share confidences.

It wasn't long before Meredith told Rose all about Adam. Rose smiled wistfully through the whole story, and Meredith suspected that she was thinking about the past, about her own memories of love and whirlwind romance.

When Meredith concluded, wondering where it would all lead, Rose leaned over and patted her hand. "Trust in your heart, Meredith and let go of your fears. When the time comes, you'll know what to do."

When Meredith offered Rose back her brooch, she simply wouldn't hear of it. Meredith couldn't understand why Rose wouldn't take the pin back. It was clearly a valuable piece of jewelry, and beyond that, it obviously had a great deal of sentimental value to her. But Rose mysteriously insisted that Meredith hold on to it a while longer. Despite Meredith's questions, she wouldn't say why, and she was so firm about it, Meredith couldn't refuse.

Meredith couldn't quite fathom the mystery of it. Yet, her relationship with Adam seemed to affect almost every aspect of her life. In some ways it was a subtle change, but people began to notice. She looked different, acted different and even felt a new wave of inspiration and expression, in both her work at Colette and her own artwork. Adam never seemed to stop telling her that she was wonderful and even beautiful—praise that made her head spin. In his arms she did feel wonderful, treasured and unique. The more she revealed of her true self, the more beautiful Adam seemed to find her. As her parched ego soaked up his admiration, she felt herself thrive and blossom.

When she looked back now at her relationship with Jake Stark, she questioned if she had ever been truly in love. She'd been infatuated with Jake, and awed by his reputation. But she'd never once shared the special sense of connection she now felt with Adam. Each time they made love, her desire for him grew even stronger.

She never worried anymore about being an inadequate lover. His sighs and groans of satisfaction were assurance enough. The more he responded to her loving touch, the bolder she became, surprising herself as she devised uninhibited and creative ways of pleasing him. Making love to Adam seemed to draw out a side of herself she'd never known existed. She had never responded to Jake the way she did with Adam…and doubted it could be as wonderful with any other man.

She did worry sometimes about the future. Where was it all leading? Aside from her own fears and doubts, she worried that Adam was hurt more from his marriage than he even realized. One night, as they lay side by side, talking, he more or less confirmed her suspicions, revealing that Suzanne had actually betrayed him and left him for another man. Although Meredith couldn't see his expression in the dark, the heartrending tone of his voice was proof enough that the wound was still fresh.

She held him in her arms and tried to take away the pain. She understood so well how he felt. She would never dream of hurting him that way. Yet, would she end up disappointing him just as badly someday?

Though he'd never said outright that he loved her, when he spoke of the future, she was clearly included in the picture. She liked to daydream about being Adam's wife, what a wonderful fantasy that was. How lucky she'd be...and how proud. But she also caught herself up short before getting too carried away.

Adam wanted children. He wanted them very much. There was no mistake about that. But she was not cut out for motherhood...and never would be. So it seemed to her an insurmountable obstacle they'd be forced to face one day. She didn't like to look that far ahead. When Meredith was away from Adam, she could summon up a long list of reasons why it wouldn't work between them and why she should end their relationship before she got her heart broken. She knew Adam had helped her overcome a burden of insecurities. But going a step further, like falling in love... The idea was just too frightening to her.

Yet, when Adam was near, his merest smile melted every doubt. She loved being near him, hearing his voice or meeting his compelling gaze. Merely watching him walk across a room gave her a secret thrill. She knew she would never grow tired of looking into his dark eyes.

When worries flocked around her head and threatened to shadow her happiness, Meredith tried to remember

Rose's simple words of advice and to trust that if the time came to decide whether or not to leave Adam, she'd know in her heart what to do.

With Adam's encouragement—and a bit of nagging—Meredith finally drummed up the courage to call David Martin. Meredith wondered if he would remember her, but he clearly did. Obviously a man who had little time for chitchat, the gallery owner quickly arranged a date to visit her studio. When Meredith hung up the phone, she shot up from her seat and jumped straight up in the air, clapping her hands. Adam of course was the first person she called to share the news, and he sounded excited.

"He's coming by on Saturday morning," she explained. "I'm so nervous. Can you be there with me, Adam?" Meredith asked on impulse. She was usually so independent and self-sufficient, the question was a surprise even to herself.

"Of course. If you want me to," he replied, his voice touched with a note of wonder.

"I do," she said firmly. Before meeting Adam, she would never have asked anyone to be present at such an important interview. But it was different with Adam. He was just…part of her now. She felt as if she absolutely needed him there.

She could almost hear him smile.

"I'd be honored. And when he offers to exhibit your work, we'll open a bottle of wine and drink to your success."

"Oh, Adam, please," she wailed. She sat down again and held her forehead with her hand. "Don't say things like that…you'll make me even more nervous."

"Sorry," he replied with a laugh. "But I will bring that wine."

When the big day arrived, Meredith also felt it necessary to bring Lucy along, which made Adam laugh as the big dog piled into the small back seat of his sports car. Meredith often brought Lucy to the studio with her, especially when she worked there late at night. Partly just for company and partly for protection, though Lucy was much too friendly to be a real watchdog.

David Martin arrived exactly on time. Many artists had studio space in the warehouse district, and he was quite used to navigating the narrow, winding streets. The meeting started off pleasantly and if David was surprised to see Adam present, he didn't show it. Today the gallery owner was dressed in black from head to toe, a finely tailored sports coat, crew-neck sweater of thinly knit fabric, black jeans and boots. His work clothes, Meredith suspected. The somber, totally hip outfit was intimidating and made her even more anxious.

With a dazzling smile he accepted her offer of refreshment, choosing a bottle of spring water. Then it was down to work. He pulled out a pad and a compact 35mm camera and began to survey her work with an amazingly somber demeanor. Meredith had never seen an art professional take her work so seriously, and the process made her feel as if she might jump out of her skin.

Meredith could barely breathe as she watched him slowly study each sculpture, then take photos from various angles. She squeezed Adam's hand until she saw the poor man actually wince. She finally couldn't stand it anymore and excused herself, claiming that Lucy needed a little walk.

Adam stared at her curiously and then knowingly. She had a feeling that this time, he wouldn't offer to do the task himself. ‘‘Okay, but don’t go too far,’’ he suggested, walking her to the door.

David didn’t even seem to notice her departure. Meredith didn’t know if that was a good sign…or a bad one.

Once she had walked Lucy around the block, she grew too curious to find out what was going on and immediately led the dog back to the studio. When she joined David and Adam it was apparent that David had finished. She could barely force herself to meet his gaze, knowing that once she did, he would start to talk about her work…and reveal his ultimate verdict.

‘‘There you are,’’ David greeted her. ‘‘Meredith, your work is absolutely wonderful. It’s so fresh and original. Really unlike anything I’ve seen,’’ he stated. The look of pleasure and surprise on his face confirmed that his comments were sincere.

Meredith didn’t know what to say. She hadn’t expected a flat-out rejection, but some stinting praise and encouragement, with the final message being that she wasn’t quite ready to be shown in a gallery. She was totally shocked by his compliments.

‘‘I told you she was great,’’ Adam said proudly. She felt his arm around her shoulder, giving her an encouraging squeeze. She was glad for the support as she felt a little light-headed taking it all in.

‘‘Thank you, David. Thank you so much,’’ she managed at last.

David flashed a wide smile at her. ‘‘Nonsense, I should be thanking you for inviting me here. Or more accurately, thanking Adam,’’ he added, glancing at Adam.

But his gaze quickly returned to Meredith. He was fairly beaming at her, his blue eyes sparkling. She noticed again that he was quite handsome, if one’s taste ran toward fair-haired men who looked like magazine models. Which she didn't much care for, actually. He looked like the type who was used to charming his way through life, she thought, and she was sure his looks and personality helped a great deal in his business...and with women.

"So, does all this mean that you're going to include Meredith's work in the group show?" Adam asked.

Meredith was glad that he'd voiced the question. She hadn't the courage to bring it up. She held her breath, waiting for David's answer.

He paused, turning to look at the sculptures again and then back down at his notes. "Well...that depends," he said finally. Meredith's spirits plunged at the hesitant note in his voice.

"They're not quite at a professional level...is that it?" she said.

"Oh, no. Not at all." He shook his head, then ran his hand quickly through his hair to smooth it back into its perfect, casual arrangement. "I was wondering if you'd be interested in having a show of your own. Maybe in January."

"My own show?" Meredith repeated, unable to quite believe what she'd heard.

"Fantastic!" Adam said, squeezing her shoulder.

"I have to speak to my partner about it, but I'm fairly certain it can all work out. He takes care of business matters and leaves selecting the artwork to me," David explained. "You will have to work very hard up until then. I'll need a few more pieces for the gallery space. Do you think you can manage it?"

"Yes, of course. I'll work night and day if I have to," Meredith promised him.

"Well... I hope it won't come to that. We don't want

to burn you out right before we make you a star,'' David said with a smile.

''Meredith has some wonderful smaller pieces that she keeps at home. Maybe those would be suitable to show, as well,'' Adam suggested.

''Yes, that sounds like a possibility,'' David said. ''Maybe I could come by sometime soon and take a look. How about one evening after work?'' he asked Meredith.

''Anytime. Just give me a call. I'm usually home by six,'' she said.

''Great. I'll call you next week and let you know more.'' David gathered up his belongings and prepared to go. ''I'm very excited about your work, Meredith. I have a feeling that it will really appeal to our clientele.''

''Thank you...I mean, I hope so,'' Meredith said. Adam walked him to the door, and Meredith stood in the studio feeling a bit dazed. She couldn't quite believe what had just happened. Was she really going to have her own show in a well-known art gallery? It seemed like a dream...yet it was true.

When Adam returned, his smile was a mile wide. He stood before her and she practically jumped into his outstretched arms, then hugged him so tightly he begged for mercy.

''Thank you, thank you, thank you!'' she practically shouted at him.

''It's wonderful news, isn't it? But I didn't do much. I only brought you and David together. Your own talent did the rest,'' Adam assured her.

Meredith tilted her head back and looked up at him. ''Yes...but you believed in me. And that's what made all the difference,'' she told him.

She'd always felt special around Adam from the start.

But now, finally putting it into words, she realized that Adam was the first person in her life who had truly believed in her, who had stood in her corner and given her unconditional encouragement and support. The opportunity to show her work in a gallery was an obvious change in her life brought about by Adam. But in so many subtle ways, her life and personality had been affected by his attention and loving support.

"If you give me half a chance, I'll always be there for you, Meredith," he promised. He stared deeply into her eyes, and their jubilant mood suddenly turned to one quite serious and intense. Meredith felt as if he was asking her an unspoken question. A question about commitment, about their future together. She didn't know what to say and answered impulsively by moving up on tiptoe and giving him a deep, long kiss.

Adam did not need any more encouragement than that to respond to her totally. Their kisses grew deeper and longer, and as Adam's hands lovingly caressed her body, Meredith felt that their clothes were an annoying barrier. She helped him as he pulled her sweater over her head and slipped her jeans down her long slim legs. She soon had his shirt and jeans off, too, and they moved to a cot in the corner of the studio and sought warmth under a patchwork quilt.

The blanket was hardly necessary and soon tossed aside as their lovemaking grew ever more heated and passionate. Meredith always marveled at the way it was when she and Adam made love. Each time seemed different, yet better than the last. The more familiar she became with his body and the more adept she'd grown at giving him pleasure, the more pleasurable and exciting it was for her, as well.

Soon Adam sat up against a pile of pillows, and she

sat facing him, her legs around his waist. His dark head tilted forward and he lifted her breasts to meet his warm lips. His tongue swirled and tantalized her nipples until they were taut and tingling, moving from one to the other and back again. She felt the pleasure building and building inside her, and her head arched back, giving him even freer access. While his mouth pleasured her above, his fingers moved against her warm, womanly center. Every nerve ending felt electrified, and Meredith moaned with pleasure. She felt a hollow, aching emptiness that only Adam could fill and quickly lifted her hips until she felt him move inside of her.

Adam's mouth met hers in a deep, soulful kiss, and his hands held a firm grip on her waist, moving her in rhythm to his powerful thrusts. The feeling was pure, mindless pleasure, electrifying every atom of her being. As his masterful lovemaking rocked her body to new heights, she slowly opened her eyes and met his deep, dark gaze. She felt as if they had truly merged, defying physical boundaries and united in heart and spirit. She had never before felt so close to anyone, so cherished and desired. As Adam's lovemaking lifted her to the sparkling, shimmering heights of ecstasy, Meredith knew that she truly loved him as she would never love anyone again.

Later, as they lay close together on the narrow cot, they talked about Meredith's show, and she once again marveled at her good fortune. "I'll have to spend a lot more time in the studio, I guess. We won't be able to see each so much in the evenings for a while," she reflected. "Will you mind?"

"Don't worry about me," Adam said, smoothing back her hair with his hand. "This is your big break. You've got to work hard. Give it your all. Believe me, I understand,'' he assured her. ''I remember when I was trying to build my business. I really needed to spend a lot of long nights at the office. We were so short-staffed that sometimes I'd do paperwork all day and then drive a truck all night, making deliveries. I know it was hard for Suzanne. But we both knew it was only temporary. She made me feel so guilty, you'd have thought I was hanging out with the boys all night, or seeing another woman.''

So there was another reason his marriage hadn't worked out, Meredith realized. She knew that she would have been more understanding of his pressures and maybe even tried to help him. But it didn't seem the time to talk further about his ex-wife.

''Well, you can come and visit me here sometimes,'' she suggested. ''I can take a work break.''

''If this is your idea of a work break, ma'am, I'll be there,'' he teased her, nuzzling his face into her neck. ''You always find ways to surprise me, Meredith,'' he added.

''Adam...be serious,'' she laughed. She felt herself blushing all over. It was the first time she'd ever initiated lovemaking between them, she realized, and the experiment had been an unqualified success. How bold and daring of me, she thought with a secret smile. What will be next?

''Actually, I was thinking of you being alone here at night. I know you bring Lucy, but you know as well as I that she's no watchdog.''

''Yes, I know,'' Meredith agreed with a grin.

''I'd like to get you a cell phone. And I don't want you to argue with me about it,'' he insisted. ''I'll make all the arrangements. But I want you to have it here, handy at all times. I don't want to worry about you, okay?''

She'd thought about getting a cell phone for the studio, but had just never gotten around to it. The way some people used portable phones, taking them out in the movies or library, really annoyed her. But in this case it did seem practical. A few weeks ago she would have balked at the way Adam insisted on getting her one. But now the gesture made her feel cared for, so she didn't even argue with him.

''Whatever you say, Boss.''

''Now you're talking,'' he teased her back. He gave her a firm swat on her bottom. ''I like my women... amenable. Eager to please,'' he added in a lordly fashion.

''Oh, really? What a coincidence. That's the same way I like my *men,*'' she replied in an imperious tone.

''Okay, I can do that.'' He pulled her close and growled the words against her neck. Meredith barely had time to draw a surprised breath before his hands were once again working the most wonderful magic on her body.

''Is this what you had in mind?'' he whispered in her ear.

She sighed with pleasure, her entire body growing limp against him. ''Hmm...exactly.''

Eight

All of Meredith's friends were very excited to hear her news, and their heartfelt good wishes made her feel great. Her work at Colette on the Everlasting Collection was also going smoothly, along with her relationship with Adam, which seemed to get better every day. All in all, Meredith felt as if her life just couldn't get any better.

Even the takeover rumors around the office had died down. Marcus Grey hadn't made a major move in weeks. The optimists speculated that gaining the necessary shares was more trouble than he'd expected and that he had lost interest in his prey. The pessimists around the office held a different view: they believed that the corporate barracuda was just lying low, trying to lull Colette into a false sense of security before moving in for the kill. They predicted he would pounce soon, probably around the holidays, when everyone was distracted and least suspected it.

Thanksgiving was quickly approaching, and even Meredith felt pressured to make some plans. She was already spending every spare minute at her studio and secretly wished she could stay there night and day over the long weekend, immersing herself in her artwork. But she knew that plan was unrealistic. For one thing, the Thanksgiving holiday was her favorite, even more so than Christmas, since she didn't have to shop. She even liked to try her hand at cooking and over the years had perfected a very tasty fresh-cranberry relish and a spicy pumpkin pie.

As she'd expected, her mother had invited her to visit her condo in Malibu for the long weekend. Even though Meredith had never enjoyed a close relationship with her mother, she had always hoped that once she was an adult the situation could change. Now that she found herself involved in a serious relationship with Adam, she actually did wish to see her mother and even ask for some advice. But maybe that was merely a hopeful dream, she realized, as she spoke to her mother on the phone one night. While her mother urged her to visit, she rattled on in her usual self-involved way about her friends, business contacts and her many plans and social obligations. Meredith realized that as usual they would spend very little time alone. Her mother would have the house filled with guests over the holiday, night and day. Or Meredith would be dragged along to parties at the homes of her mother's many friends.

When she finally managed to work in a word about herself and told her mother about the upcoming show of her sculptures, her mother sounded very pleased and proud. She insisted that she would come out to Indiana for the opening and couldn't wait to share the news with all her friends. At least I've given her something to brag about, Meredith thought with a wry grin. When it came to committing about the holiday, Meredith put off a final decision. She'd already told her mother about Adam and said that she wanted to check with him first, to see if he had any plans, since she didn't want to leave him alone over Thanksgiving.

The reason was mostly true, and not merely a convenient excuse. Yet, even though she felt totally close to Adam in so many ways, she hesitated to bring up the discussion of holiday plans. The topic seemed to move their relationship into a bona fide ''serious'' category, and admitting that made Meredith very nervous.

She was sure now that she loved Adam. Loved him with all her heart. How could she not? He was the kindest, most gentle, loving and compassionate man she'd ever known. He was also so intelligent and hardworking, a self-made success. And the most wonderful lover, sexy and strong, totally possessive and commanding, just when she wanted him to be. He made her feel treasured and protected, as well as respected and admired.

He was everything a woman could ask for...and more.

But that was just the problem to Meredith's way of thinking. Despite all of Adam's affection and encouragement, she still believed that she was not the woman for him. He deserved someone different, someone better, she thought. A woman with more poise and confidence, who could really be a help to him in social settings and business situations. A woman more from his circle, not a semibohemian jewelry designer who barely knew where to shop, how to dress or how to make polite cocktail conversation.

More important, she could never give him the family

he so desperately wanted. Maybe meeting her was a good and necessary experience for him, she reasoned. Undoubtedly he had helped her, but she had also helped him, for she believed that their relationship had truly enabled him to get past his divorce and try again for the life he really wanted.

But that still didn't mean that she was the right woman for him, and Meredith worried endlessly that very soon they would be forced to face this ultimate question.

Since Meredith carefully avoided talking about Thanksgiving, it was Adam who finally brought up the topic. He had persuaded her to take a night off from visiting the studio and after work had lured her to dinner at Crystal's, where they had gone on their first dinner date.

Adam had even thoughtfully arranged for them to be seated at the same table. He was nothing if not sentimental, Meredith thought when the host seated them.

"I realize it might be short notice, but if you have no plans for Thanksgiving, I'd like to ask you to come with me to Wisconsin, to meet my family," Adam said.

Meredith glanced up at him, and the rare, vulnerable look in his beautiful dark eyes made her heart melt. She bit down on her lower lip and stared at her wineglass. She knew how much Adam's family meant to him. He was close to his parents and sisters, and she admired that so much. She had seen photographs of his family and heard so much about the Richards clan, young and old, that she felt almost as if she already knew them. She was very curious to meet them all in person. She was sure that Adam's family would have a wonderful, traditional celebration, the kind that she had missed out on as a child and now couldn't get enough of as an adult.

Knowing how much he valued their opinion, the invitation was not casually issued. Adam was not the type of man to ask just any woman to come and meet his family. If he offered such an invitation, she had no doubt that his intentions were serious. Meredith was practically positive that for Adam such an invitation was tantamount to an actual marriage proposal—or perhaps, setting the stage for one.

All these thoughts flew through her head in an instant. She could feel Adam watching her, waiting for her reply. She hesitated and took a sip of water.

"I know it's short notice," he said suddenly. "Until today I wasn't sure that I'd be able to spare the time to join them. But my folks sounded so disappointed when I said I might not make it. I rearranged my schedule and moved some out-of-town trips up in my schedule.... But maybe you already have plans?" he asked politely.

"My mother has asked me to come out to California," Meredith explained. "She even sent a ticket."

"Oh, so you're going out to see her?"

"Well, I might," Meredith answered hesitantly. She honestly didn't think she was going to visit her mother, and she didn't want to lie to him. She loved him too much. "Then again, my mother's idea of a Thanksgiving dinner and mine are so radically different, I think I just might pass. The last time I spent the holiday with her, she served sushi and Martinis poolside. Oh, yes...I think there was a bottle of cranberry juice somewhere on the bar. In case any of the traditionalists wanted a cranberry vodka drink," she added with a smile.

"Sounds...very California," Adam replied. "So, you're not going out there after all, then?"

"No, I don't think so," Meredith replied honestly. "But I was thinking I might just stick around here and camp out in the studio. I've an awful lot of work to do before the show,'' she added.

''Really?'' Adam looked quite disappointed. ''Can't you spare a few days off? I hate to think of you all alone on the holiday.''

That was exactly the way she felt about him. But now she knew he wouldn't be alone; he'd be with his family. Playing with his beloved nieces and nephews. It was just as well. She couldn't bear to see what a great father he'd be, and she was sure she'd be so envious of his happily married sisters. Hopefully, their company would soothe any disappointment Adam might feel at her rejecting his invitation.

''Oh, I'll be okay. Maybe I'll get together with Sylvie,'' she added. Sylvie didn't have any family or a current boyfriend, and they hadn't seen each other much over the past few weeks. Maybe it would be good to get together with her friend and cook up their own Thanksgiving meal. Sylvie would know just the right things to say about Adam.

Meredith could feel a certain foreboding that, at that very moment, things were turning around in her relationship with Adam. Just the quizzical way he was looking at her gave her knots of dread in her stomach. It was the start of the end. She felt it in her bones, and there was no way around it.

Adam reached across the table and covered her hand with his. ''Meredith, lately you've seemed a little... distant,'' he admitted. ''I know you're distracted, getting ready for your show. I really understand that. But about Thanksgiving, are you really too busy to come, or just worried about meeting my family?

Meredith took a deep breath. ''I am worried. But more about what your invitation means.''

"Oh...and what does it mean to you?" he asked quietly.

"That our relationship is serious."

"Don't you think it's serious?" he asked, looking genuinely puzzled. He took his other hand and folded both around her own.

"I—I'm not sure. I'm not sure I'm right for you, Adam," she admitted.

He looked genuinely surprised, but when Meredith searched his expression for some sign of distress or anger, she found none. Only patient understanding, which touched her heart.

"Right for me? You please me and feel right for me in every way possible. How could you ever think otherwise?"

She looked down. She knew this conversation would be hard, but she had never imagined how hard. He just couldn't understand. He didn't want to, she realized.

When she didn't answer right away he said, "Aren't you happy with me? I thought you were."

"I am," she assured him, suddenly looking up again to meet his gaze. "I'm just confused, maybe," she admitted. "I know we're happy together. Divinely happy," she added, "but I worry about the future. I'm not sure I can give you...what you need. What you deserve," she added in a quiet, but emphatic tone. She wanted to say, I can't give you a family, children. I'd be a terrible mother, I'm sure of it. I'd end up disappointing you so badly you'd probably come to hate me.

But she just couldn't make that confession to him. She couldn't say anything at all.

He gazed at her thoughtfully, but didn't respond right away. Finally he squeezed her hand. "Why don't you let me worry about that. So, you won't be able to come with me for Thanksgiving,'' he added. ''Don't worry. I understand. Maybe next time.''

She glanced at him. ''Yes, maybe next time,'' she agreed, feeling sure that there wouldn't be a next time.

But Adam was nothing if not persistent and determined; an unflagging optimist. He'd promised her once that she wouldn't get away from him easily. Now she was beginning to understand just what he had meant by that vow.

After dinner they returned to Meredith's apartment, and when Adam took her wordlessly into his arms in her darkened bedroom, she felt as if she wanted to cry for some reason. She loved him so much. It was hard to feel it all falling apart around her, as if the very ground was giving way beneath her feet. She returned his kisses fiercely and passionately, making love with him that night with a depth of emotion she hadn't dreamed possible.

The next morning they left the apartment in a rush, so there was no chance to talk any further. As Adam had mentioned, in order to fit in his visit to Wisconsin he had to be out of town on business for several days over the next week. He was leaving later in the day and would be gone until the middle of the next week. He would have one day back in Youngsville before he left to visit his family, the day before Thanksgiving.

Meredith knew she would miss him terribly. She recalled the trip he'd taken out of town for a few days, right after they had first met. Her every thought had been shadowed by his image, and the days apart had seemed endless.

It would be even worse this time. But he said he would call her every night, and she knew he would keep that promise. She tried not to dwell on sad thoughts of missing him and chose to see this time apart as a chance to work at her studio. After all, she had to get used to missing Adam, for it seemed very clear now that sooner or later he would be gone from her life.

It was hard to keep from thinking about Adam and their future—or lack of it. Meredith tried to focus on her work at Colette. Almost since the day she'd met Adam, she hadn't been her usually productive self. So far, her boss hadn't said much about the deadlines she'd missed, or her bouts of forgetfulness. But Meredith knew it was time to bear down and catch up. She caught up on the schedule for the Everlasting sample pieces, which were now in a revision stage.

She also got back to work on some smaller projects, including the stickpins and key chain medallions she'd designed for Adam's company. She took even more pleasure in the assignment than she had at the start, since she wasn't just doing her job, but creating something for the man she loved. She planned to show Adam the revised samples of the pieces she'd designed for him when he returned and hoped he'd be pleased.

Meredith did use the night hours after work productively, and the next two nights she stayed in her studio until nearly midnight. Adam reached her on her new cell phone and was concerned, of course, about her late hours. Their conversations were brief and somewhat unsatisfying, she thought. They were both very tired after a long day's work. Adam especially sounded drained and more distant than she had ever heard him. All they could really talk about was how much they missed each other. She kept expecting Adam to bring up Thanksgiving again, but she was relieved that he never did.

His third night away, Adam was surprised to find her at home when he called. It was noisy in the background and sounded as if he was calling from a pay phone somewhere, perhaps a restaurant, she thought.

"Meredith? It's me," he greeted her.

"Adam, hi. Where are you? I can hardly hear your voice," she told him.

"I'm calling from a restaurant. We had to entertain some buyers tonight, and I knew I wouldn't get back to the hotel until very late. I'm glad to see you took a night off from the studio. I think you need the rest," he added.

"Yes, I did need a break," she admitted. But there was another reason Meredith had needed to stay home. David Martin was visiting, to look at her small sculptures. He was, at that very moment, wandering around her living room, doing his notepad and camera routine. Taking his time about it, too, she thought. She was tired and didn't feel like entertaining.

"David Martin is here," she told Adam. "He came to see the smaller pieces. To see if he can use them in the show."

"Yes, he mentioned he needed to do that," Adam said. Did he sound unhappy about David's visit? It was hard to say. The background noise was very loud, and she strained to hear his reply. "Well, tell him I said hello, would you?"

"Of course," Meredith said.

"I won't keep you, then, if you're busy," Adam said abruptly. "Besides, sounds like I'm losing the connection. Can you still hear me?"

"A little..." Meredith did hear a lot of static, too. "Well, goodbye. I miss you," she added in a softer tone.

"Me, too," he said. Then he said good-night, and Adam was gone. Meredith stared at the receiver a moment before clicking it off. When she turned to see what David was up to, she realized that he'd been watching her. He smiled and then looked down at his pad, making a quick notation.

"Was that Adam?" he asked.

"Yes, he's away on business for a few days. He said to say hello."

"Tell him I said hello back," David replied. He was smiling again, displaying his perfect white teeth. But something in his wry, ironic tone rubbed Meredith the wrong way.

"I will." Meredith stood up and walked to the far side of the room, to put the portable phone back in place.

"Does he call you every night while he's away?"

Meredith found the question surprising. What business was it of his? "Yes, he does," she replied firmly.

"How sweet," David remarked. "I guess it's serious between you two, then?"

Meredith now felt wary at the direction of his questions. She didn't want David's romantic interest and felt she'd done nothing to encourage it. She knew that now was the time to make it clear to him that she had no interest in him that way. If it meant losing her show, so be it.

"Yes, our relationship is serious," she stated in a confident tone. "Very," she added for emphasis.

Then she suddenly found it ironic that she was so willing to assure an almost perfect stranger of her commitment when she was not willing to state her feelings nearly so clearly to the man she loved.

"That's good," David said. He raised his hands as if she'd been arguing with him about something and he wanted to show that he was not going to fight. "How nice for you both. You make a great couple," he added.

"Thanks," Meredith said politely. "So...are you finished? I have to be at work early tomorrow."

"Yes...yes, of course," David replied. He glanced at his watch. "Wow, look at the time. I had no idea I'd been here so long." He slipped his pad and camera into his leather satchel and headed for the door. Meredith felt relieved to see that he was leaving. She walked ahead and opened the door for him.

"Oh, by the way," he said, just as he was about to go, "my partner, Tom Pendleton, would like to meet you. It's customary when we're mounting a show for an individual artist. I thought we could all have dinner together sometime...say, this Friday or Saturday night?"

Adam wouldn't be home until next week, so she was free for the weekend. Yet, she wished that Adam were home so that he could accompany her. David's attention had made her uncomfortable tonight, and she found the thought of having dinner with him and a stranger rather intimidating.

"I'm not sure...could we do it next week perhaps?" she asked.

"Next week is a holiday weekend," David reminded her. "Tom will be out of town, and I'm scheduled for a trip myself to visit some artists in New Mexico," he explained. "It really is important that you meet with Tom," David added. "He's very curious about my latest discovery."

His tone was cordial, even lightly humorous, but Meredith felt the subtle pressure. "All right," she said. "How about Saturday night then?"

"Perfect," David replied with a wide smile. He named a very hip, downtown restaurant a block or two from his gallery and asked her to meet them there at the bar at half past eight.

When Meredith finally closed her front door, she breathed a sigh of relief. Watch what you wish for, she reminded herself. You just might get it. She'd never imagined that finally achieving some recognition for her artwork would involve so much socializing and jumping through hoops. Yet, she knew as an unknown quantity she was in no position to make demands, or appear uncooperative to David, who had been great to have given her this chance.

The dinner with Tom Pendleton went more smoothly than Meredith had imagined. Tom was about David's age, but small, dark and very intense, the complete opposite of his business partner in looks. He had a more serious personality than David, but he was also quite friendly. Both men seemed to know everyone at the fashionable eatery and both talked nonstop about the art scene, nationally and what was going on in Europe.

It sounded to Meredith as if running the gallery involved a great deal of travel for both of them. For David in particular. It wasn't as if he actually bragged about the glamorous and interesting life he led, but the message was clear to Meredith.

After college Meredith had made it a point to keep up with news in the art world by visiting galleries and reading the art scene magazines. While she mostly listened as they both spoke, she added informed comments here and there which she knew impressed both of her dinner companions.

Later they asked about her work at Colette and admired the amethyst and silver jewelry she was wearing and had designed.

"You see," David said, leaning back in his chair, "she's amazingly talented. Maybe we should also show some of her jewelry," he told Tom.

Tom smiled. "I think we can start with the sculpture

for now.'' He glanced at Meredith. ''We don't want to overwhelm our clientele.''

''Of course not,'' Meredith replied politely.

She wasn't sure what to say. Keeping up with their conversation tonight had been exhausting. She was hoping that one of them would soon ask for the check. She didn't want to miss Adam's call tonight. She had a lot to tell him.

Finally Tom asked the waiter to bring the bill. David turned and asked if she wanted a ride home. Meredith knew Amber Court had to be out of his way since he'd mentioned living in this neighborhood, near the gallery. But she didn't have a chance to answer. Her cell phone in her purse rang insistently, and she pulled it out to answer the call.

It was Adam. She felt so happy to hear his voice, even though the restaurant was so noisy it was hard to hear him. ''Adam? I can barely hear you,'' Meredith said. She turned her back to the table and covered one ear with her hand.

''Where are you? Not at the studio,'' Adam replied with an edge to his deep voice.

''I'm having dinner with David and his partner, Tom,'' Meredith explained. ''David wanted us all to meet. We're just about to leave, actually.''

She knew that both men could hear her conversation, so she couldn't be as frank with Adam as she wished. She could hardly tell him now that David had pressured her to accept the invitation, or any of her impressions about the pair. It had been a draining night and she longed to confide in Adam. But it would all have to wait.

''Well, I'm glad I caught up with you, then,'' Adam replied.

"Can I call you back a little later? I should be home soon," Meredith said.

"No...I don't think that will work out. I'm in Seattle tonight, remember? It's only eight o'clock here. I'm going out to dinner. I won't be back to the room until late." He sounded hurt that she wasn't able to keep up with his agenda. But he was in a different city every day. It was hard to keep track.

"Maybe tomorrow then," she offered. "I'll be in the studio all day."

"I'll be traveling all day," he said. "But I'll try to call at night."

"Okay," Meredith said quietly. She wanted to tell him how much she missed him and how she couldn't wait to see him again. But she felt self-conscious with David and Tom just inches away. "Good night, Adam. I'll talk to you tomorrow then," she said.

Adam said good-night, his voice sounding a bit warmer and more tender, she thought. More like the Adam she was used to. Then he hung up.

Meredith sighed and closed the phone. Tom had just signed the check, and the waiter was leaving the table.

"Something wrong?" David asked solicitously.

"No...not at all," Meredith assured him as she dropped the phone into her purse. "Thank you both for a wonderful meal. It was great to meet you, Tom," she added.

"Great to meet you, too, Meredith. David had spoken so highly of you, I told him that I just had to meet this woman," he said with a laugh, glancing at David. "But you're all he promised and more."

Meredith felt herself blush at the compliment, but tried to ignore it. "Well, thank you again for taking on my work. I hope it does well for you."

"I know it will," Tom assured her.

"I have no doubt," David said, flipping back a lock of his long, blond hair with his hand. "Are you questioning my taste, Meredith?"

"No, not at all," she replied with a laugh.

The two men rose, and David helped her with her chair. They chatted some more as they left the restaurant, and once outside, Meredith had to insist on taking a cab and not accepting David's offer of a ride.

When she got home, she called Adam's hotel in Seattle and asked for his voice mail. She knew he'd already gone out, but she wanted to leave a private message for him, telling him how much she missed him and how she couldn't wait for him to get home.

The next day Adam called her in the studio. Her voice mail message had pleased him and everything seemed back to normal between them. They talked for a long time, ending with some fake kisses over the phone that got Meredith so distracted she had to take a long walk with Lucy outside in the brisk fall air before being able to get back to work again.

Adam was due back on Tuesday, on an early-evening flight, and Meredith had offered to meet him at the airport. At first he'd argued that it wasn't necessary for her to come all the way out there after work, but when she insisted, he gave in, sounding flattered by her eagerness to see him.

She honestly couldn't wait.

Nine

On Monday night Meredith worked late at her studio, trying to finish up the first phase on a new piece before Adam returned on Tuesday. She had missed him so much, and now he would be back for only one day before another long separation over Thanksgiving. Meredith was beginning to wonder if she'd been too rash in refusing his invitation to go to his parents' home in Wisconsin. She'd mentioned the problem to Sylvie, Lila and Jayne, and her friends had encouraged her to go. Maybe if they talked more about her true concerns for their future, her friends advised, Adam would understand.

Just as Meredith pondered these serious questions, a visitor buzzed outside the studio. She carefully checked to see who it was and found David on the other side of the heavy metal door.

"David, what are you doing here?"

"Oh, I was just in the neighborhood, visiting another

artist and I saw your light on,'' he said. ''Mind if I come in?''

''Uh…no. Not at all. I was just finishing up for the night and about to go home,'' she explained.

Lucy went over and sniffed at David's leg.

''Oh, you bring your dog here often?'' he noticed.

''She's good company,'' Meredith replied.

''How cute.'' David leaned over and gingerly patted Lucy's head. ''Good dog,'' he murmured. Meredith could tell he didn't really like dogs and was just performing for her benefit. Lucy, bless her, seemed to sense it, as well, Meredith thought. Normally she would have offered a visitor some coffee or a soft drink, but for some reason she didn't want David to get too comfortable.

She moved back to her sculpture and began cleaning up. ''Is there anything you wanted to talk about? About the show, I mean?'' she asked, still curious about his visit.

''No, not really.'' He drifted around the studio, looking at her work and sketches. He was wearing a thin, form-fitting black turtleneck and a leather jacket with blue jeans. He kept the jacket on and dug his hands in the pockets. She could feel his gaze fixed on her as she worked, but she didn't look up at him. She knew she looked awful, but for some reason she didn't care. She was dressed in her usual studio attire, paint-splattered denim overalls, with a ragged T-shirt underneath and a man-size flannel shirt on top. Her hair was pinned up on her head in a haphazard construction of clips, designed to keep it out of the way from the blowtorch. She also wore her large, tortoiseshell glasses, since her eyes were irritated by the chemicals and paints used for her work. Hiking boots and a complete lack of makeup completed the look.

"Is Adam back from his trip?" he asked.

"He'll be back tomorrow night. I'm picking him up at the airport."

"Are you really?" David said, sounding surprised. "Can't he find a cab?" he joked.

"I want to meet him," she said, meeting his gaze.

He leaned back against a countertop and crossed his arms against his chest. "Yes, it's a serious relationship. I remember you told me that."

Meredith glanced at him, but didn't reply. She felt as if he was trying to goad her in some way. Intuitively she felt the wiser course was to simply ignore him and end their meeting as suddenly as it had occurred. She decided to skip the rest of the cleanup, grab her coat and just leave.

"Meredith, I know I don't know you well, but I do consider you a friend. I've been thinking about your relationship with Adam, and honestly, I feel concerned," he said.

"Concerned? About what?" she asked in a surprised tone. Oh, dear. She hadn't escaped fast enough. Here it comes, she thought.

He took a step toward her, his head tilted to one side as he spoke. "Well, for one thing...don't you think that Adam is maybe...a bit too old for you?"

"Too old?" Meredith pulled on her jacket. "Don't be silly. We get along perfectly," she told him.

"You do now, of course. Everyone gets along great at the start," he said knowingly. "But ten, fifteen years from now you might feel different."

Meredith drew in a harsh breath. The man had some nerve. She clipped on Lucy's leash and grabbed her knapsack. "Thanks for your concern. But I really don't think you ought to worry about how I'll be feeling ten or fifteen years from now, David,'' she said curtly. ''I think it's time to go. You first,'' she instructed him. ''I have to shut the lights and lock up.''

''All right.'' If he was embarrassed by her reaction to his unsolicited advice, he didn't show it, she noticed. Thick skin, to go along with that flowing head of hair, she thought.

She stood near him by the door and flipped off the light switches. She thought he would take the hint and walk out ahead as she'd instructed, but he didn't go.

''I'm sorry if what I've said makes you uncomfortable, Meredith,'' he said, talking softly to her in the dark. ''I know Adam has done a lot for you...but things are going to change for you very quickly now.'' He reached out and touched her shoulder. ''The truth is, I can do even more to help you with your career.''

Meredith was so shocked by his insinuation, she didn't know what to say. Light from the street filtered through the windows, casting his face in shadows. He looked as if he was about to lean forward and kiss her, but she couldn't be sure.

She quickly moved past him and pulled open the door, hoping to flee.

As the door swung open to the street, Lucy yanked on her leash and barked. Meredith looked up and felt her heart skip a beat when she found Adam standing on the sidewalk, just outside the door. A cab at the curbside was just pulling away.

She pressed her hand to her chest. ''Adam! You nearly gave me a heart attack. What are you doing here?''

Lucy's leash fell from her hand and the dog ran straight to Adam and jumped up on him. As Adam ruffled her fur, Lucy gave him a big lick on the chin. He beamed at Meredith. ''I managed to get out of Chicago early. I wanted to surprise you.''

''I'm so happy to see you,'' Meredith exclaimed. She moved toward him and put her arms around his neck. Their lips met in a deep kiss, and she couldn't keep from sighing out loud.

But as Adam lifted his head and looked past her, she felt his body tense. ''David...what are you doing here?''

Meredith had almost forgotten about David. She let go of Adam and turned around. David stood in the open doorway, smiling that cool, knowing smile of his that was starting to get on her nerves.

''Ah, the wandering hero returns, bag and baggage,'' David remarked in a grand-sounding voice. Meredith hadn't noticed before, but Adam did have his briefcase and large traveling bag piled at his feet. He'd obviously come straight from the airport by taxi.

''Yes, here I am. Adam to the rescue,'' Adam replied dryly.

''Nothing to fear, old friend. I was just visiting with Meredith,'' David explained with a shrug. ''How was your trip?''

''Excellent. I got a lot accomplished,'' Adam answered curtly.

''Good for you,'' David remarked as he strolled past them and into the street.

''Good night now,'' David called over his shoulder as he walked toward his car.

Adam and Meredith both said good-night in return. Then Adam turned and gazed down at her. She felt disturbed by his questioning expression and immediately felt self-conscious, as if she had something to hide. When in fact she had done absolutely nothing wrong.

She decided to ignore Adam's curious stare and try to

get their reunion back on track. "You must be very tired."

"I'm beat," he admitted.

"Then let's go home, and I'll take care of you," she said. She leaned over and picked up his briefcase, and he slung his suitcase strap over his shoulder.

A short time later they were in Meredith's apartment, where they dumped all the luggage at the door. Without even bothering to put on a light, Adam pulled her close and immediately began pulling off her clothes. Meredith's eagerness to feel his bare skin pressed to hers, to touch him and love him, easily matched his own. They were soon in her bedroom, stretched across the bed in a torrid, loving embrace. She'd never been ready so quickly to have him inside her, and he'd never moved so fast before to make them one.

As she felt them come together she sighed with heartfelt pleasure. Adam groaned, and with his hands on her hips, pushed her even closer. Then she closed her eyes and let go and lost herself in the mindless, endless joy of loving him.

They made love furiously, fell into a deep sleep, then woke again in the middle of the night to make love at a tender, leisurely pace. When bright sunlight filtered through the bedroom curtains the next morning, Meredith woke slowly. She felt as if she wanted to sleep all day, but she knew she couldn't. The space beside her on the bed was already empty. Adam was an early riser, no matter what. She smelled coffee and felt grateful that he'd made it. It made it easier for her to get up and join him.

"Good morning, sleepyhead," he greeted her warmly. He had on a dark-blue wraparound robe that set off his looks perfectly, she thought. Seated on a tall stool at the kitchen island, he was sipping coffee and reading the newspaper. He'd already showered and shaved, his dark hair wet and slicked back, emphasizing the rugged lines of his handsome face and strong jaw.

She couldn't resist putting her arms around his shoulders and testing his smooth cheek with her hand. "Hmm, like a baby's bottom," she teased him.

She felt his hand on her bottom then. "Exactly," he remarked.

She laughed and moved away from him. She poured herself a cup of coffee and sat on the stool directly opposite. Her hair fell across her eyes, and she felt Adam reach across and brush it aside. His hand lingered on her cheek.

"I missed you," he said again, perhaps for the tenth time since he'd returned. Not that Meredith had been counting. She'd told him the same just as often, if not more. "I missed seeing you in the morning like this."

"With my messy hair and squinty eyes?" she laughed.

"And your froggy morning voice," he added. "I like that part the best, I think. You sound awfully sexy," he added.

"Adam, how can that be sexy?" she asked, sipping her coffee.

"I don't know. Everything about you seems sexy to me," he admitted with a devilish grin. She reached across the counter and took his hand.

He gazed at her lovingly and Meredith felt perfectly content. "I've been thinking about our talk the other day, Meredith," he admitted in a quiet voice. "In fact, I thought about it quite a lot while I was away."

"You mean, about joining you for Thanksgiving?" she asked. If he invited her again, she would go.

"About that, sure... But more about what you said after, about feeling unsure about our future and doubting that you're right for me."

"Oh, yes, I remember," Meredith replied. She felt a cold chill of dread and pulled her hand away from his.

"I had a lot of time to think while I was away," he said as he rose from his seat and came around the counter. "I realized something," he said. "Something very important." He stood just inches away from her and placed his hands on her shoulders.

"What was that?" her mouth grew dry as she stared into his dark eyes.

"I realized that I've never told you how much I love you. How much I truly, deeply and utterly love you."

His expression was so sincere, so utterly beautiful, Meredith felt her soul melt. "I love you, too," she said in a whisper. "I love you so much."

He pulled her close and kissed her, a deep, hungry and possessive kiss. Finally, he pulled his head away and looked down at her. "I want you to marry me, Meredith. I know we haven't known each other for very long. But I feel so sure about this. So certain that we were truly meant to be together. I know you have your doubts, but there's nothing we can't work out together," he assured her. "Please say yes and say you'll come with me to Wisconsin to meet my family."

Meredith felt stunned. As if she'd been on a roller-coaster ride, rising giddily with Adam's confession of love, and now, crashing down a long, terrifying hill with his proposal.

She pulled away from him and walked into the living room.

"Adam...this is all so sudden. I don't know what to say," she answered hesitantly.

"Just say yes," he urged her in an upbeat tone. "We know we love each other. And we know we can't stand to be apart.... What more is there is to figure out?"

She turned to face him. "A lot more," she said sadly. "There are other things to think about. I love you with all my heart," she promised him, "but that still doesn't solve everything."

He moved toward her, looking genuinely puzzled. "What is there to solve?" Then his eyes narrowed, and the look on his face nearly frightened her. "It's David Martin, isn't it? You're seeing him...or you want to," he accused her coldly.

"Adam, don't be ridiculous! There's absolutely nothing going on between David and me. And there would never be, whether I knew you or not."

"I wish I could believe that," Adam said, looking hurt and angry. "But it's all starting to add up. The way you've become so distant lately. So distracted. Your refusal to come with me to Greenbrier. Why, almost every time I called you last week, you were with him, and even last night it was almost midnight and he was with you at the studio."

"He surprised me. I didn't invite him there," Meredith assured him.

"What, is it because he's younger? Or do you feel that you're already outgrowing me?" Adam asked. He turned his back to her and paced across the room. "Like a butterfly, coming out of her cocoon. Now that you've found your wings, you're off to better things. Is that it?"

"Adam..." He was so upset. Meredith had never seen him like this. Usually he was the one assuring and comforting her, but now the roles were completely reversed. She walked up behind him and gently rested her hands on his back. "Adam, please. Don't do this," she urged him. "David means absolutely nothing to me. How can I make you believe me? If you asked me to give up the show and never speak to him again, I would."

Adam's dark brows drew together, his eyes narrowed as he stared at her. She could tell that her words had penetrated and he was finally starting to believe her.

"You'd do that for me?"

"Yes, if you asked me to. If it would make you believe that nothing has ever happened between David and me."

He sighed and pushed his hands through his hair. "I'd never ask you to do that, Meredith. And I do believe you," he admitted. He turned away from her and stared out the window. "I'm sorry for doubting you. A knee-jerk reaction from my marriage, I guess," he explained. "But that still doesn't explain the reason you won't accept my proposal."

"My reservations about marrying you have nothing to do with David or my career or anything you've said so far."

"Then what is it?" Adam turned and faced her. "You owe me a real explanation, don't you think?"

Meredith stepped back and took a deep breath. It was hard for her to confess her true fears to him, especially in his dark mood. But she knew she must.

"Adam, I'd love to marry you. I imagine sharing a life with you all the time, I really do," she began. "But I don't want to have children, and I know that having a family is so very important to you, something you've dreamed about. From what you've told me, it seems like that issue was part of the reason your first marriage didn't work out."

Adam looked stunned. He swallowed hard. "Yes, I

guess that's true enough...but you've never told me you don't want children, Meredith.''

''Well...we've never really discussed it before, have we?'' she pointed out. ''I think you just assumed I shared your view...or maybe you think that every woman wants to be a mother.'' She sighed and sat down heavily on the couch. It was so hard to talk about this. He must think her a terrible person now, not to want to have children if she could.

''But why...because of your career? We could have all the household help you wanted, Meredith. You could leave Colette and just do your own artwork once we were married.''

''Oh, Adam. It's not that I don't want your children. I fantasize about it, how wonderful it would be. I really do,'' she admitted, her eyes welling up with tears. ''But I'm terrified of being a mother. I know I'd be just terrible. My own mother never gave me any example of what to do. How to give a child the loving care kids really need to grow up right, I mean. I'd make a mess of it. I know I would. I'd end up disappointing you, and you'd end up hating me,'' she predicted.

''Meredith...'' He dropped to his knees beside her and put his hands on her shoulders. ''I could never hate you. What are you saying? You'd be a wonderful mother. Why, look at the way you take care of Lucy. You treat her like a baby, and she's spoiled rotten,'' he added with a small smile, trying to lighten her mood.

His argument did make sense, but it was hardly enough to break down her granite-hard, lifelong fear. ''Oh, Adam...'' She cupped his cheek with her hand. ''Please believe me...'' She shook her head sadly and began to cry again. ''I'd do it if I could. But I just can't.''

He pulled her close and drew in a long, deep breath. She felt his tender hands on her back and in her hair, soothing her. ''Don't cry, Meredith. Please,'' he urged her. ''I'm trying hard to understand, honestly,'' he said. His voice was so rough she wondered if he was about to cry himself. When she finally pulled herself together and put her head back to meet his gaze, she could see that her guess had been correct. His eyes were glazed, filled with unshed tears.

She lifted her hand and touched his cheek. He covered her hand with his own and kissed her palm, then placed it back in her lap. He stood up and took a deep breath. ''I guess I'll go dress,'' he said. ''I'd better get into the office.''

''Yes, of course,'' Meredith said. She sat there, feeling stunned as she watched him go back into the bedroom. The morning had started off so wonderfully bright, but now, despite the brilliant sunshine outdoors, it felt black as midnight.

Meredith dragged herself through work that day. Over lunch she confided her problems to Sylvie, who offered friendly support but no real solutions. Meredith was truly grateful just to have her friend hear her out. She knew that no one could solve this problem for her. She had to figure it out for herself.

When she came home that night, she met Rose in the lobby, just about to leave the building. ''Meredith, how are you? I've seen so little of you lately. You must be working awfully hard for your show.''

''Yes, I've been at the studio every spare minute,'' Meredith confessed.

''I can't wait to see your new work. I'm sure it's wonderful,'' Rose said encouragingly. Then she gave

Meredith a searching look. ''You look tired, dear. I hope you're not running yourself down.''

Meredith knew that she looked absolutely awful today. She'd been crying off and on since the morning. Her eyes were red rimmed and shadowed by dark circles. She felt exhausted and just wanted to fall into bed and go to sleep.

''I'll be okay,'' she promised Rose. ''I'm going to turn in extra early tonight.''

''Good, sleep is a wonderful thing. It's an amazing cure-all,'' Rose remarked. ''Is Adam still out of town?''

Meredith averted her gaze and shook her head. ''Uh, no. He got back last night. But he's leaving again tomorrow, to visit his parents in Wisconsin.''

''Oh?'' Rose looked surprised. ''And you're not going with him?''

''He asked me to,'' Meredith confessed. ''But I decided not to.''

He's even asked me to marry him, she wanted to add. But for some reason she just couldn't. She'd tell Rose sometime, she was sure. But not yet. The pain of their exchange was still too fresh.

''Oh,'' Rose said with a curious look. Meredith thought she was going to ask her more questions, but she didn't. She pulled on her hat, an attractive bright-blue felt fedora with a wide, soft brim that suited her perfectly. ''If you have no plans, I'd love to have you down at my place,'' Rose said. ''Sylvie will be there and Jayne and Erik, and the twins,'' she added. ''Lila and Nick may even come. It'll be great fun,'' she promised.

''All right,'' Meredith said. ''Thank you for inviting me.''

She really couldn't stand the idea of being alone all

day, now that there was so much trouble between Adam and herself. "How about if I bring a pumpkin pie?"

"Terrific. That's my favorite," Rose replied.

They said good-night and, just as Meredith had planned, she went up to her apartment and went right to bed.

Meredith didn't hear from Adam that night or the next day. She had finished the stickpin and key chains for him and considered sending the pieces to his office. If he were any other client, she would have. But she didn't want it to look as if she was forcing him to call her and decided to keep the pieces over the holiday weekend. Then she'd be in touch one last time. On Wednesday she jumped every time the phone in her office rang. Then in the late afternoon she realized that he must have left for the airport and would not be calling her to say good-bye.

Had they already broken up and she just couldn't face it? she wondered. Maybe she would never hear from him again. She couldn't expect to refuse a marriage proposal from a man like Adam and have him return to grovel. He certainly wasn't going to beg her to marry him. She was sure of that.

On Wednesday night she returned from the supermarket to find a message from David Martin on her answering machine. She was surprised to hear from him. She'd wondered if her reaction to his advances had made him angry. Angry enough to change his mind about showing her work. But she'd been too focused on Adam to give much thought to that question. Without Adam in her life, the show didn't seem very important. She hardly cared what happened.

But David sounded friendly and businesslike and left

some dates and instructions about delivering her sculptures to the gallery.

It seemed her questions were answered. David was going to pretend that nothing unusual had happened that night in her studio and he was giving her the cue that she should do the same. As for her show, it seemed that all was going according to schedule and he wasn't going to let their personal relationship—or lack thereof—affect their business plans.

He added that he'd be away on business for the next few weeks but if she had any questions, she could contact his assistant. He then added that he hoped she and Adam had a good holiday.

Now, there was an irony, Meredith thought. She was looking forward to the unhappiest holiday she'd had in years.

On Thanksgiving morning, she set about baking her pie for Rose's party. The task gave her some distraction from her low mood, but at the last minute she felt like making some excuse and hiding away in her apartment the whole day. But she knew Rose wouldn't let her do that. She finally dressed and went downstairs at one o'clock.

Sylvie, along with Jayne and Erik, were already there and greeted her warmly. Wonderful, tantalizing aromas of turkey and stuffing and all the trimmings floated out of Rose's kitchen and made Meredith's mouth water.

Rose soon bustled out of the kitchen in her apron and greeted Meredith with a warm hug. Then she pulled back, with a startled look on her face, and Meredith realized that Rose had been struck by the brooch on her dress.

"Oh, Rose, I purposely wore this pin today so I wouldn't forget to give it back. Now you must let me return it to you,'' Meredith insisted. She lifted her hands to the pin and started to remove it.

''Don't be silly. You keep it on, just for today, Merri,'' Rose urged her. ''It looks wonderful on that dress, and I'd much rather admire it on you, then stick it in a drawer somewhere. Besides,'' Rose added, ''I'm thinking of loaning it to Sylvie. I'll give it to her later, after dinner. She's always admired it, and now that you, Jayne and Lila have all borrowed it, I've decided she should have a turn.''

Once more Meredith gave in to her friend but secretly promised herself that by the end of the night she'd return the pin, whether Rose argued with her or not.

The gathering of good friends and good food proved to be just what Meredith needed to take her mind off her breakup with Adam. Still, Adam's image was never very far from her thoughts, and she sometimes drifted off, distracted from the conversation as she imagined him in Greenbrier, surrounded by his family.

As the meal drew to a close, the talk at the dinner table turned to the takeover at Colette, and Meredith was suddenly drawn into the discussion.

''I've heard he's bought up more shares,'' Sylvie said in a deeply concerned tone. ''It won't be long now.''

''Maybe someone will figure out some way to stop him. Isn't there some legal position the company can take?'' Lila asked.

''Yes, the corporate attorneys are working on legal strategies to block him,'' Jayne offered. ''But he's tricky. He seems to outthink them at every turn.''

''I wonder what motivates a man like that?'' Nick asked. ''I mean, what makes him tick?''

''He obviously can see he's going to make so many people miserable if he succeeds. But he doesn't seem to care,'' Sylvie cut in. ''His motives must be very deep,'' she added. ''And he must be a perfectly miserable man.''

''Yes,'' Meredith agreed, thinking her friend was very insightful. ''I've wondered about that myself,'' she added.

''Oh, now, enough of this doom-and-gloom talk, everyone,'' Rose insisted from her seat at the head of the table. ''It may turn out well in the end after all, you know.''

''You know what they say in baseball,'' Erik offered, ''It ain't over till it's over.''

Rose laughed. ''Well, this feast isn't over until we've all eaten our fair share of dessert. Now, who will help me bring out the coffee and pies? I think there's one for each us.''

''I will, Rose,'' Meredith offered rising from her chair. She knew the socializing had been good for her, but she hoped that after coffee was served she could soon slip away from the gathering.

Just then the doorbell sounded and Rose went to the intercom in her foyer. Meredith heard her speak briefly to her visitor, then buzz the front door open.

Was Rose expecting another guest? She hadn't mentioned it, but she had so many friends, perhaps some more visitors were coming for dessert. As Meredith arranged china cups and saucers on a tray, a knock sounded on the front door.

''Meredith, would you get that, dear?'' Rose asked. She was at the stove, checking on an apple pie that was warming in the oven.

Meredith went to the front door and pulled it open.

''Adam,'' she said abruptly, ''I thought you went to Wisconsin.''

Then she couldn't speak. A giant lump was lodged in her throat.

"I did. But I turned around and came back."

He stared down at her intensely, and she could feel his dark gaze just about penetrating her very soul. She felt an almost overwhelming urge to simply throw herself into his arms, but she held back.

No, she couldn't do that. She didn't have the faintest idea why he'd returned. Probably just to set things straight before they officially parted. He was not the type to just cut a woman off without explanation.

"Can we talk somewhere privately? Up at your place?" he asked.

"Yes…yes of course. Wait here a moment. I'll tell Rose I'm leaving."

She returned to the kitchen and told Rose that Adam had arrived and she needed to speak with him in private for a few minutes.

Rose didn't seem surprised at all and, of course, she had buzzed Adam in so she already knew of his surprise visit.

"Take your time. I'll save some dessert for you," she replied.

Without any of the other guests noticing, Meredith slipped out and went upstairs to her apartment with Adam. Once they got inside and shut the door, she felt her stomach knot with dread.

"You've come a long way…what do you want to say?" she asked him.

He stood facing her, looking handsome and strong… and far too wonderful to ever let him leave her life.

"That I love you, truly," he said in his quiet, certain way. "And that I want you to be my wife. I don't care if you don't want a family. I just want you Meredith. I don't think I can live without you… I know now I don't want to try,'' he confessed. ''If you'll agree to marry me, I'd be the luckiest man alive.''

Meredith felt stunned. She'd had some time to think over their problem, too, and she'd come to some new conclusions, as well. But she'd never dreamed she'd have a chance to share them with him.

She felt herself bursting into tears and raised her hands to her face. But this time the tears were tears of joy. In an instant Adam's strong arms were around her and she felt his lips against her hair. ''Meredith, what is it? Please talk to me.''

She took a deep breath and pulled back. Then she smiled at him. ''I was thinking, too, Adam,'' she told him. ''You've helped me so much. Your love and respect has made so much possible for me. For once in my life, I've been able to let go of so many fears and insecurities. And I've come to see that I've secretly always wanted to have children. I've just denied that wish to myself and let my fears control me. I want to marry you, Adam, and have children with you. I know that with you by my side, I can do anything,'' she confessed sincerely. ''And I just hate the idea of you having a baby someday with any other woman,'' she added with a laugh. ''Maybe I'm afraid of parenthood…but I just couldn't stand that,'' she added as she reached up to touch his beloved face.

''Do you really mean it?'' he asked, his expression reflecting surprise, joy…and total adoration.

''Absolutely.''

He smiled and kissed her so deeply and held her so tightly, it took her breath away. ''You're the only one for me, Meredith. Now and always.''

''As you are, for me,'' she murmured against his lips. Their kisses grew deeper and deeper, but before things went too far, Adam suddenly pulled away.

''Wait, I almost forgot. I have something for you...'' He reached into his pocket and pulled out a dark-blue velvet ring box. Meredith immediately recognized Colette's distinctive gold emblem embossed on top, and her hands shook as he gave it to her.

''Well, aren't you going to open it?'' he asked with a small laugh.

''Of course,'' she said quietly as she snapped open the lid. She had to blink twice when she saw the ring within.

''Oh, Adam...how did you know?'' she asked, in utter disbelief.

It was her favorite engagement design from the Everlasting Collection. The ring she had always fantasized about receiving when—and if—some special man asked her to marry him.

And now it had all come to pass. She'd never imagined in a million years such a vision could have come true. But since Adam had entered her life, all her deepest wishes now seemed to be coming true.

Adam took the ring and slipped it on her finger. ''Perfect fit, too,'' he said proudly. He lifted her hand to his mouth and kissed her palm. ''Frank told me it was your favorite, and he made this one for me from your design. So, will you do me the honor of being my wife, Meredith?''

''Yes, it was my favorite,'' she said, gazing at Adam and then down at the ring. ''I'll make our wedding bands,'' she told him as she took his hand and led him toward the bedroom. ''I think the group downstairs can do without us for a while, don't you?'' Meredith asked in a sexy whisper.

''They'll just have to.'' The gleam in Adam's eye and his low, husky tone totally excited her. ''Thank goodness it's a long weekend.''

Meredith laughed as he took her in his arms and playfully tossed her on the bed. ''Hmm...you're right. How convenient.''

He came to her on the bed, covering her body with his own, and Meredith closed her eyes as she met his deep, thrilling kiss.

Ten lifetimes wouldn't be enough to express her love or satisfy her desire for Adam, she realized. Their love would always be extraordinary—the everlasting kind.

Lost in their own world for the next few days, Meredith and Adam didn't tell a soul about their engagement. On Saturday they were finally ready to spread the good news. Adam called his family and put Meredith on the phone to say hello. She knew that he must have had everybody wondering what made him rush back to Youngsville on Thanksgiving morning. But Adam's folks sounded just as he had described them, warm and easygoing. Very pleased by the news, they made the couple promise to visit over Christmas.

Meredith's mother was also happy to hear about her engagement and now had two good reasons to come to Youngsville. Meredith knew that even her finicky mother would be very impressed by Adam. Maybe even surprised that Meredith had captured his heart.

When Adam left for a few hours to take care of chores at his own place, Meredith went downstairs to visit Rose. She wanted to share her good news with all her best friends at once, but there hadn't been any answer at Lila or Sylvie's apartment and she knew that Jayne had gone to visit Erik's family.

"I have some big news, Rose," Meredith said almost as soon as Rose let her in. "Adam and I are engaged."

"You are? That's terrific!" Rose enveloped her in a huge hug. Then she stepped back and grinned. "I thought something like that might be going on. I did notice his car parked out front since Thursday night."

Meredith laughed and blushed. They hadn't even left her apartment to eat.

"Yes, well...thanks for the leftovers," she replied, referring to the tasty package of turkey and trimmings that Rose had thoughtfully left at her door. "We were getting tired of take-out," she admitted. Then changing the subject, she added, "Adam even surprised me with a ring. I guess he knew before I did that I would accept."

"Oh, let me see." Rose eagerly reached for Meredith's outstretched hand. "What a beautiful design. Is it from Colette?"

Meredith nodded. "From the new collection I've been working on. He had my boss, Frank, make it up for me."

"How thoughtful. From all that you've told me, Adam sounds like a wonderful man. I'm so happy for you, Merri."

"Thank you, Rose. I can't wait for you to meet him."

"I can't, either." Rose smiled and Meredith was sure that Rose and Adam would get along perfectly. "Why don't you bring him here for dinner one night this week? I'll ask Sylvie, Lila and Jayne, too. They haven't met him, either, right? We'll have a little celebration for you."

"Please, Rose. I don't want you to go to any trouble. You've just had Thanksgiving for everyone."

"It's no trouble at all," Rose argued. "We'll keep it

simple. I promise I won't fuss,'' she added, which Meredith knew meant only that she wouldn't prepare individual soufflés or anything impossibly elaborate. ''As you get older, Merri, you realize that it's important to celebrate when you can. You four girls are like family to me. It would make me very happy to have you all here and have Adam meet everyone. Please let me?''

Rose's warm words and genuine good wishes touched Meredith's heart. Her friends at Amber Court were like family, Meredith realized. The one she'd never really had.

''Of course,'' Meredith agreed with a soft smile. ''I'm very honored, honestly. But you have to let me help, okay?''

''Agreed,'' Rose said with a nod.

Then just as she was about to go, Meredith suddenly remembered the hard little box in her pocket.

''I almost forgot,'' she said, pulling out the velvet jeweler's box. ''Here's your brooch. Thanks again for loaning it to me.''

''You're very welcome. I love seeing it put to use. Beautiful jewelry shouldn't be hidden away in a drawer somewhere, taken out only for special occasions.''

''I definitely agree. But then again, I'm in the business...and you sound as if you ought to be,'' Meredith added with a laugh.

She saw the color rise slightly in Rose's cheeks. ''Don't be silly, dear. I'm not the business type, believe me.'' Rose picked up the box and opened it, then looked down at the glittering brooch on its satin cushion. ''But I have enjoyed seeing you and the others get some use from this pin.'' She paused, and still gazing at the brooch she said, ''I think I'll loan it to Sylvie next. She's the only one who hasn't had a turn.''

"Yes, that's true, isn't it?" Meredith suddenly realized that Rose had so far loaned the brooch to Jayne, then Lila and then herself. It only seemed fair that now Sylvie had a turn.

Rose snapped the box shut and set it back on the table. "I'll give it to her next time I see her," she said decisively. "It might lift her spirits. She's been feeling so worried about the takeover situation at Colette."

"Yes, she's really taking it to heart," Meredith agreed. "More than most, I think." Meredith felt a sudden pang of guilt. "I've been so wrapped up with Adam and getting ready for the gallery opening, I haven't really been there for her lately," she admitted.

"Don't feel bad," Rose said as she reached over and patted Meredith's hand. "That's exactly the way it should be when you fall in love. The rest of the world sort of disappears," she noted with a laugh. "I'm sure Sylvie understands." She glanced at the box with the brooch again. "If she doesn't right now, she certainly will when it happens to her."

"I hope so." Meredith thought of the happiness and deep love she'd found with Adam and wished the same could happen for Sylvie, too. "I hope she meets someone she likes soon," Meredith added. "She deserves the best."

"Of course she does," Rose agreed. "But I've found that you can't chase happiness. You have to wait for it to find you. But I do have a feeling it will find Sylvie very soon."

Meredith met Rose's gaze and once again, found that mysterious sparkle in her knowing gaze. A look that made her very curious about Rose's past and how she'd come to be so wise.

Someday Rose might reveal her secrets, Meredith

thought. This time however, Meredith was content to answer Rose with just a smile, wondering if her friend's intuition about Sylvie would really come true. She certainly hoped so.

* * * * *

Turn the page for a sneak preview
of the final 20 AMBER COURT *title,*

RISQUÉ BUSINESS

by award winning author
Anne Marie Winston on sale in
December 2001 in Silhouette Desire…

And don't miss any of the books in the
20 Amber Court *series,*
only from Silhouette Desire:

WHEN JAYNE MET ERIK, September 2001
by Elizabeth Bevarly

SOME KIND OF INCREDIBLE,
October 2001
by Katherine Garbera

THE BACHELORETTE, November 2001
by Kate Little

RISQUÉ BUSINESS, December 2001
by Anne Marie Winston

One

Sylvie Bennett closed the door of 4A and headed down the stairs of her apartment building at 20 Amber Court. As she reached the head of the sweeping marble staircase that led to the foyer, her brisk pace slowed. Through the leaded glass panes surrounding the front door, she could see fat white snowflakes falling over Youngsville, Indiana, her hometown.

Great, she thought in disgust. A lake-effect snowstorm was the last thing she needed today. Normally she enjoyed walking to work rather than taking the bus. But today she wanted to look particularly crisp and professional. Chapped cheeks and wild, wind-whipped hair didn't fit that profile one little bit.

Sylvie's normally buoyant spirits sank even lower as she thought about what she intended to do today. She was entirely likely to be trudging the long blocks home without a job tonight.

"Sylvie! Good morning!"

Her morose mood vanished at the sight of her landlady, Rose Carson. A pretty flannel robe covered Rose's curves, and her salt-and-pepper curls were tousled as if she hadn't bothered to brush her hair yet. She looked warm and approachable and...totally huggable, thought Sylvie whimsically. If she'd ever dreamed of having a mother, which she hadn't allowed herself to do in a very long time, Rose would fit the bill. She treasured their friendship.

"Hi. How are you this morning?" Sylvie descended the steps and crossed the foyer to Rose's door, where the older woman stood with her newspaper in hand.

"I am marvelous," Rose said brightly. "I have a feeling something wonderful is going to happen today!"

Sylvie smiled wryly. "That would be nice." She began to wrap her woolen scarf snugly around her neck.

"That's a lovely suit, dear." Rose reached out a hand and gently smoothed the fabric of one lapel. "But, if you'll forgive me, I think you need something striking to set it off."

"Probably," Sylvie agreed. "But what good jewelry I own would fit on the head of a pin."

Rose's eyes twinkled. "Shame on you, young lady! You work for one of the most prestigious jewelry houses in the country and you don't have any of your own?" Her eyes lit up, and she raised a hand, indicating that Sylvie should wait a minute. "I have just the thing."

"Rose, you don't have to—" But her landlady had dashed back into her apartment before Sylvie could complete the sentence. She was back within the minute.

"Here we go." Rose held up a stunning brooch fashioned of precious metals. Several pieces of clear golden amber glittered amid a cluster of other gems. Although it wasn't quite heart-shaped, Sylvie's first thought was that Rose was giving Sylvie her heart to wear.

"I couldn't possibly—oh, it's beautiful." Sylvie inspected the piece in the hall mirror. "This is spectacular. Where did you find it? Who made it?"

"A designer I knew a long time ago," Rose said, dismissing the topic. She reached forward to position the brooch against Sylvie's lapel. "This is exactly what you need today."

"Oh, I couldn't. It's too valuable—"

"And it does nothing but gather dust in my jewelry case," Rose interjected. Her nimble fingers fastened the pin in place. "There, look how stunning that is." She took Sylvie's shoulders and turned her to the mirror hanging on a wall in the foyer.

"It *is* perfect, isn't it?" Sylvie touched the brooch with a gentle finger. She needed all the self-confidence she could get today. Perhaps she would borrow this from Rose, just this once. "All right." She turned with a smile, leaning forward to press a kiss to Rose's smooth cheek. "You win. I'll wear it."

"Perfect!" Rose clapped her hands together like an excited child. "You'd better get going, dear. I know you like to get into the office early, and it will be a little slippery today, judging from my window."

Sylvie nodded as she finished winding her scarf around her mouth and neck, and donned her long winter duster. "Wish me luck. I have an important meeting today." Well, that wasn't a lie. The fact that she hadn't exactly been invited to the meeting was beside the point.